First published in Great Britain 2014 ISBN:
978-0-9926196-4-0

Published by:
The Wacky Wordshop.
40 Emmerson Way
Hadleigh,
Suffolk
IP7 6DJ

http://thewackywordshop.co.uk

Cover illustration: Copyright Kevin Thomas

Printed and bound by Amazon CreateSpace

Fear your past ... Fear your future.

It's a grey morning in the city of London, a predictable day for all ... but one. Amelia Gizzard discovers her twin sister has fallen victim to murder, leaving a daughter behind ... the young June Gizzard. Unable to come to terms not only her sister's death but also the behaviour of others around her, Amelia seeks answers.
But when June exceeds the bounds of reason and reveals her true colours, Amelia must escape. Now the subject of a criminal enquiry Amelia must salvage past memories and piece them together. Can she do this while being hunted by the police, and pursued by her family's evil history? Will she return to her roots to uncover what has been kept from her for so many years, or will she share the same fate as her sister?

Kevin Thomas.

I have been reading for as long as I can remember. Writing followed in primary school years. I have written short stories and the odd poem, but never thought of writing a book until my teen years, eventually completing my novella. A good friend suggested I find a good publisher. So I did.
It has been a long process of proofreading, editing, tweaking and preparing Forgotten Truths to be the best it can be. Without the help of many people I couldn't have done it. I am truly grateful for their goodwill and effort. I am still young, so my writing is constantly shifting in style, and improving as time goes by. This is my first published book, and I will always be proud of it because it's my ambition realised. I hope you enjoy reading this as much as I have enjoyed writing it.

Judgements

An electric vibe permeated the room, its four walls embracing one event - assassination. Detective Amanda McIsaac searched for any evidence pieces which might offer up traces of DNA or semen, or which may have been overlooked by the forensics team. Whoever it was, the killer had made certain to leave no trail. But, even the best are often caught at their own game.

In the centre of the room lay the corpse of a female, arms and legs splayed. Her head had been tilted back, sightless eyes wide open. Masses of soft golden hair sprawled out behind her, floating in a sticky red liquid. Her mouth was slightly ajar, as if she'd been about to utter her last words. Booted, bloody prints lead from the head to the front door, out into the city of London.

Amanda held her nose, stepping carefully over the body. Unlike newcomers to the force, she wasn't at danger of being weak. She'd learned over many years to suppress her nightmares and the ever present side effects that followed her cases; it was a tough way of living, but business was business. She knew she hadn't been the first to arrive on this grim, frosty morning. She'd been in mid-conversation over the phone with her Aunt Hayley, discussing arrangements for the next Christmas and why she still didn't have a husband. "Because men are all the same!"
"You're only saying that because of what happened. When are you going to learn? You can't run from the past forever?"
"Oh, Auntie Hayley ... hang on, I've got another call."
The sight of the slim figure, standing with both hands on the door frame jolted her back to reality. It was the one

man she'd dreaded seeing ... Detective Charles Fisher. Amanda swore sotto voce and turned away. They'd been lovers in the past. Picnics in the setting sun, thoughts of having a family. On the night they were due to pack for a long trip to Colorado she'd caught him in bed with another woman. Her cousin. From then on her life had spiralled out of control.

Enough was enough. She'd confided in him how her mother had died at birth, how she'd been raised by her sweet aunt, but bullied and abused by her cousins with whom she'd had to share a home, a school and a life. All her life she had been 'marked' as 'different' but from her eighteenth birthday had gone straight into training, then on to become a homicide detective. Why? Because it made her feel superior. She thrived on helping people, enjoyed being 'someone' rather than 'no-one'. It was the cousin who'd beaten and spat at her on her way home from school. He'd shared a bed with one of the people who'd destroyed her self-esteem, scarring her forever. Charles Fisher knew that once he'd hopped into that bed he'd never again share love with Amanda McIsaac. A year later she'd found herself transferred all around the country, from base to base, each time meeting new and different people. Each time, just when she found herself settling it would arrive, the dreaded e-mail notifying her official transfer. She knew it was because she was the best in town; she was good, no one could doubt that. But it was always so sudden. She was beginning to feel more and more isolated and the job ... well, it wasn't what it used to be. Whilst packing for London a warming thought had struck her, "Maybe this time will be different?" Little did she know she was about to be placed under the same roof as Charles Fisher, the man who'd not only cheated on her, but single-handedly torn her life apart. And taught her one thing only … to trust no one.

"What have we got Amanda?" Charles approached casually.

"Bullet to the head, two stab wounds to the neck. Brutal."

Feeling uncomfortably close to him she edged away. He raised an eyebrow. "Something the matter?" *How dare you, you bastard.*

"Not at all." She forced a weak smile.

"You're telling me. No one heard… not even next door?"

"No one. Can't blame people across the street. Next door's old folk so …" Her voice trailed off. Amanda wondered, 'Someone must have seen or heard something?'

"Pensioners, hard of hearing," murmured Charles. She nodded.

"This killer's bad ..." She continued. "Not like our usual cases. I mean, come on, do you really think this poor girl stood any chance?"

She didn't need an answer.

"Any sign of a struggle?" "None."

"So, fill me in; I need more information if we want to catch this bastard." He spoke with eagerness, a strange excitement.

"We think there's a possibility she was brought here before she was killed, the killer may have spent a short time with her."

"Abducted?"

She nodded. "The woman living next door but one claims she saw a red Mercedes with tinted windows leaving the victim's house around 21:00 hrs. That's all we have so far." Charles stroked his chin, his five o'clock shadow visible, even under the dim light.

"Phone?"

"Yep, Nokia N78. We're tracing all calls dialled over the past two weeks ... may lead to something, but I doubt it."

"You're right. I doubt someone this good would leave a phone behind, but it's a possibility. Any family members, friends, work partners? And I'm guessing we know the victim?"

"Emma Gizzard had one teenage daughter - June, a sister Amelia, and both parents - still alive. Apparently she wasn't much of a 'goer outer' if you know what I mean? She usually kept to herself."

"It's going to destroy them." He was right. It was always tough informing a family that their loved one had been murdered. Amanda knew everything about the business. Inside and out. How would she convey the truth to Emma Gizzard's family? One thought that never left her mind was ... how would she feel in their shoes?

"I should go find the sister then?" Amanda nodded towards the door.

"Yeah, that'd be great. See you soon." She didn't reply. Outside, the assembled media forced her to shield her eyes from the cameras flashing in her face. 'Be appropriate when answering questions, and feed just enough information to be left alone.' She reminded herself to prevent a lash out. Her main priority was to find Amelia Gizzard, the sister of the victim.

Through the mass of reporters, camera men and news vans she spotted a small figure matching her description. The figure was head to head with a circle of guards, thrashing her arms and hissing. Amanda's walk soon turned into a worried jog, until she'd reached the spot where the main gates to the flats were situated.

"Let me in, that's my sister in there!" Amelia cried out, fighting off the guards. Amanda wondered, 'Now how does she know?'

"Amelia Gizzard?" Amanda placed a soft hand on her shoulder. Amelia shoved the press away and came quickly forward.

"Who's asking?"

"I'm Detective Amanda McIsaac. Would you come with me, please?" She smiled politely, masking her true feelings.

"No. Tell me here ... first. What's going on? Is my sister okay?"

"Miss Gizzard, please, just step ins ..."

"Tell me if my sister is okay. Just ... please tell me." Her soft expression was on a highway to rage.

"Amelia I ... I'm so sorry. Your sister has been killed." She hated bearing bad news, especially in public; it was never her style.

"Don't say it." Amelia fell to her knees, tears pouring from her eyes. It couldn't be true ... could it? Em, her little sis, dead?

"We need your help in every way possible, to arrest whoever did this." Amanda offered a supportive hand, yet all the while suspecting her of some connection to the murder.

"This way Amelia." She motioned her over to a black Ford Focus. Its windows were tinted.

It took a few moments before Amelia stepped forward, her face blank. The room they travelled too was hushed; its bare white walls enough to drive one to insanity if left to sit for any length of time.

"Coffee?" Amanda offered. It bore a strong resemblance to winter mush.

"No."

"Something to eat?" She continued her polite pretence.

"No."

"Okay." Amanda reasoned physical contact wouldn't help. She understood Amelia's need to get away – if she was innocent.

"Just tell me how my sister died?" Amelia demanded.
"We're not certain yet; waiting for the pathology report."

Amelia leaned forward. "Tell me what you know." Her voice was rough and Amanda could see her arms shaking on the metal desk.

"She was murdered, Amelia. Kidnapped or abducted ... Well, we believe she was ... from where we don't yet know." Amanda paused, the next few words dangling on her tongue. "She was shot in the head and stabbed several times. I'm truly sorry."

§

1992, Ridgewood farm.

The lava lamp rested straight and proud on her bedside table, its soft violet glow dimly illuminating the room, limiting her sight. Straining her ears she was barely able to make out the sounds of wheat blowing about in the wind. She thought it strange the way the weather worked on the farm. The animals would surely be asleep by now?

She rubbed her head, exhausted. Still half in dreamland she swung her legs from under the covers. Slowly she climbed from the bed, rubbing her eyes. The wooden floor creaked beneath her feet. Creeping on toes made no difference to the creaking noises giving away her position. She squinted, but it was no use. She knew that the wire leading from the lamp was there somewhere and that she daren't catch her foot on it; it would wake her parents for sure. What a Christmas present ... half a year earlier she'd sat cross- legged in the living room, drowning out the voices of her wealthier cousins as they ripped apart their presents, stacked in piles. She'd received one that year.

"What's this?" she'd squeaked, trying her best not to notice her parent's look of worry at being dry when it came to money, embarrassed at their daughter's only gift.

"It's a lava lamp." Her mother smiled nervously. Amanda scrunched her face up ready to cry, instead falling into her mother's arms and whispering two words.

"It's beautiful."

Amanda rolled her eyes at her gift of lying. She'd acquired it as a little girl; handy at times, at other times the main cause of a family row. But why had she woken up at this hour of the night? Her knee collided with the corner of the dresser. Loud curses erupted from her lips. Stumbling backwards she felt a thin wire brush her skin. It happened before she could do anything. She glared miserably as the lamp slid from its place and bounced on the wooden floor. She'd figured it could survive. Until the second bounce. It shattered, spilling its purple contents all over the polished floor. The 'bang' was still ringing in her ears as she braced herself for screams and lectures, all the while grabbing at the bigger bits of glass for disposal.

Suddenly she was wide awake. Through the fog of her mind it hit her … *no screams from across the hall*! The bang that had lingered in her hearing was not from the lamp; it had come from downstairs. That was what had disturbed her sleep. Willing herself on she stepped over the liquid and on into the darkness to investigate the noise. Glass bits tightly in her hands she opened her bedroom door and stepped out into the narrow, black hallway; shuddering as her bare feet felt the chill of the wooden floor. The door to her parent's room had opened ever so slightly. Odd? The door was kept shut at all times, day or night …

She crept on through the upper floor halls. It was a large house, barely manageable. The farm had always raked in a substantial amount of money but, sadly, when it came to the paying of bills, food, and materials for the farm's benefit, the McIsaac family were very limited. Things like 'treats' and luxuries' had never appealed to Amanda, she'd been raised that way. It was the norm to just 'survive' and 'scrape by'.

In the corner next to the landing she could have sworn she saw the outline of a skinny man, but quickly dismissed the thought and continued on to her parent's room. She tapped lightly three times, fearful of a lecture. After a long three minutes in the cold hallway she knocked again; again no answer.
"Here goes nothing." She murmured under her breath. Amanda furrowed an eyebrow as she stroked the creaseless silk sheets. They were lavender fresh; clearly the bed hadn't been slept in.
"Mum?" She whispered, confused. It was wrong, all wrong. Not once had her parent's sleeping pattern ever gone awry, their timetable ever broken. Had they gone out for some urgent reason? Maybe some fresh air? Highly unlikely. A gentle wind drifted in through the open bedroom door. Despite its mildness it sent shivers up her spine. Suddenly she felt overwhelmed; total loneliness, like a child who's lost its mum in a supermarket. It was difficult leaving the comfort of her parents' bedroom, yet she knew she'd have to search deeper in the house to find them. Where could they really have got to? She chuckled with a nervous shake of the head, admitting she was over- reacting. Then she heard the static crackle, an uncomfortable sound, a sound that signalled danger. She knew immediately it was the antique television set downstairs, permanently unplugged. It had been plugged in. By who's hand?

12

§

She scrambled down the stairs, heading towards the light shining at the bottom. Obviously, her parents had wanted to watch television. She grinned as she skipped the final step and stumbled into the bright room. Her heart dropped. Two figures seated in front of the television, each bound a wooden chair. Beaten to a pulp. "Mum, Dad!" Amanda cried, running forward. Her mother's eyes flickered. She mumbled something, some sort of warning. It was too late as two large hands threw her roughly to the floor, pinning her in place.

"Do you like what I've done to Mummy and Daddy?" A calm, velvety voice whispered.

"Let me go! I'm not afraid of you!" Amanda screamed.

The voice chuckled. "You might not be, but Mum and Dad certainly are."

"What are you going to do to them?" The click of a cigarette lighter froze her blood; she smelt petrol. Her helpless parents were soaked, head to toe, terror and desperation in their eyes.

"Guess." The voice hissed.

§

 Amanda McIsaac had never been keen on London. The lifestyle failed miserably to live up to her standards. Heavy traffic and loud noise wreaked havoc on her sleep – which, in her line of work she desperately needed. Bred as a country girl she'd known no other life before joining 'the force'. The farm, with its crops and breeding animals had been her safe haven; its natural wonder was like her personal drug. Until the day her parents were taken.

§

Once again she'd been transferred; this time from Liverpool. Her new friends were no more, she was alone, like always ... that's what she told herself anyway. But that's why she was here, to forget; to do what she was best at ... her job.

Amanda was sure the room temperature had been set to below freezing. She didn't mind; completely understandable for the procedure in hand. The area was tiled black. In the right hand corner stood a trolley with an assortment of tools carefully set out in size order. In the left hand corner an ancient computer stood on a shabby desk. Her eyes studied the corpse on the metal bed in the centre of the room. She stepped forward, needing desperately to touch it, to picture herself at the scene of the crime, freeze the moment the gun was fired, bring the killer to justice. She contemplated the options. Option one was that the girl had fallen foul of a random killer seeking a thrill. Option two was that she'd been caught up in a cycle of trouble: she reminded herself to enquire about signs of drug or alcohol abuse. Right now Emma Gizzard's lifeless form bore no resemblance to her twin sister. The skin was whiter than chalk, eyes closed to make her appear at peace. Amanda shuffled awkwardly closer; the body radiated cold; she shivered, lifting her hand halfway to touch the corpse, debating whether or not the skin would rupture under her touch. She decided to leave the physical examination to Rita.

Forensic pathologist Rita Rose paced the room. She was plump, in her mid-fifties, black hair permanently covering her left eye, concealing its beautiful shade of green. She was a kind person, her talents soon acknowledged after leaving university. Daily she sat, examining corpses ... except for lunch break. Despite everything she seemed mentally able to handle returning home every night with the scent of death clinging to her clothes. Amanda admired her for that. Rita chose to pace a few extra steps, shuffling her thoughts before turning to Amanda.

"I'm sorry we were sort of slow with the report," she said. "It's okay. I know how hard the job can be."

Rita took a deep breath, massaging her temples. "If you look there I have confirmed the cause of death as the gunshot wound." She said, placing a sheet of paper in Amanda's hand.

"And the knife wounds? I mean, I'm no forensic pathologist, but if you were at the scene of the crime … fuck, Rita …it was like a blood bath." She imagined a blade brutally ripping the girl to shreds.

"They may have contributed, but couldn't have been the cause of death; not deep enough into the tissue."

Amanda bit on her lip. "DNA?" A spark of hope within her ignited.

"Sadly none. In these cases you've only to take one look at the body and the violence of the attack, and your initial thoughts are 'we're gonna catch this monster'. It's natural to assume there is evidence." Charles Fisher's words echoed her ears 'I need more information if we want to catch this bastard'. Suddenly she was fearful of returning empty handed, fearful that her spark was dying out.

"So, basically…" she half asked, dreading Rita's next words.

Rita nodded slowly. "Little chance of catching the killer."

§

The day was young. A gentle breeze fluttered around the guests. Oak trees had shed their leaves. They appeared dead, fallen branches lying everywhere. It suited the funeral setting perfectly. Emotions ran high in the group, each person able to express theirs in a physical way. She knew bottling it up wasn't healthy, would only make things worse. At the same time she knew she should cry, but shock wouldn't let her. The smooth voice of Father Cromwell filled her ears like soothing liquid. Looking up was terrifying. She pretended to listen, watching the grass aimlessly, looking for a way to wake up from a nightmare which was actually reality.

"Let us commend Emma Francine Gizzard to the mercy of God. May she rest in what we hope will be peace, may her soul be one with the angels. Emma, may we remember you for what lay within you; your ambition, your politeness, your will to give to others. We commit her body to the ground; earth to earth, ashes to ashes, dust to dust; in the sure and certain hope of resurrection to eternal life." Father Cromwell's soft voice fell silent, as did those around him.

She could feel eyes on her, willing her to look up. Lifting her head she watched, heartbroken and dazed at her sister's coffin being lowered slowly into the grave. Amelia had no faith in God but needed to believe her sister was now in His hands and at rest. She bit her lip, hoping to pierce the skin and feel pain, anything but this. June's small gasp forced her back to the moment.
"What is it baby?" She whispered, stroking her niece's arm.
"Yo … your hands!" In the centre of her palm were red dotted crescents. She'd clenched them so hard that she'd cut her palms; she didn't care. The pain was soothing.
"It's fine, June." June nodded sadly, reverting her attention back to the coffin. Amelia clutched her sides tightly, reminding herself to breath. It felt impossible.

Her sister ... her twin .... far too young to have died, especially be murdered. She clasped a necklace to her chest, not wanting to let go. It was really a beautiful gem, although she wasn't entirely sure what it was. Its stone was covered in a rainbow of tranquil colours. Its warmth comforted her. Flashbacks from her past returned. She deeply regretted the times she'd muttered, 'If only she wasn't my sister'. Right now she wished it was her and not her sister buried beneath the ground, although she liked to think she still had some treasured memories left to look back on in later life.

When you cry, you cry. When your heart loses the will to beat ... that's when your emotions are real. Amelia stepped back, remorse flooding her veins, her heart beating faster. Tears blurred her vision, her stomach knotted; the previous night's food rising in her dry throat. Calm conversations became screams. Sweat trickled down her back. Her legs buckled. She buried her head in shame, her mind went blank, it felt as if she was in a dream.

§

They were on a plane ... herself, June and Emma. Outside, the sky glowed in shades of blue and crimson, clouds puffed like pillows and their parents were far from sight, no longer able to inflict pain. Reality intruded once more ... no dreams, only nightmares. Quickly her mind focused again on her niece, Emma's daughter, the real victim.

§

June Gizzard was as sweet as sweet comes. From what Amelia had once been told she was achieving top grades and on her way to becoming a fine, successful young woman. Yet every girl needs a mother. How was she, Amelia, going to handle an emotionally needy girl like June when she could barely manage her own life? But, she would do whatever it took to make her sister proud ... she had to. She had seen the way Emma looked at June, and 'proud' was the only word that came to mind. Amelia thought back to her own mother who was a strong character, radiating beauty and strength.

"Dad's mad because all the men at the pub fancy Mum." Emma had whispered gently, leaning over the balcony, puffing at the forbidden cigarette.

"I thought he didn't love her?" Amelia replied, recalling recent and frequent fights they'd had.

"He doesn't. He doesn't love any of us, neither does she. They're more alike than they think." Emma spoke bitterly.

"You can't say that!"

"Can't I?"

Emma stared blankly at her, flicking the cigarette away. She walked off. It hadn't escaped her notice that her mother hadn't attended the funeral. Most people would assume it would have been too much for her to bear. Amelia knew otherwise. Her mother was selfish. She would care, of course, but no more than she would about losing a diamond ring; it could be replaced. She had another daughter. It wasn't as though both her children had died. She'd never been there for them anyhow, hadn't seen Emma in almost a year. Apart from the rare phone call the girl had pretty much forgotten her mother. Not that Amelia blamed her sister. It had never occurred to her mother that a parent should be with her child until the end, even if meant attending her funeral. Only once the air was 'clear' with not a soul in sight could Amelia bring herself to approach her sister's grave for a final few words.

"I remember once you woke me up ... crying because Nanny had recently died. You told me you were scared of dying and never wanted to grow old. I remember telling you not to worry, that I would die first because I was older, and then I remember you saying you'd rather die first because you couldn't live without me." She wiped away a tear. The cool breeze feathered her hair, taking the flush from her cheeks.

"This is how I feel. I'm sorry Em. You were my sister. I should have been looking out for you, I'm selfish and ..." She stopped, afraid of breaking down.

"I need to know who did this. There are so many memories, bad and good. I know Mum and Dad were harsh. I know how much you hated them. You were the best thing in my life, and now you're gone. I want you to know that I will care for June as best I can. I'll raise her like you'd have wanted. I'll be back soon angel, but for now here's something to remember me by." She bent and laid a single red rose on the wet soil. Its petals floated beautifully in the wind. Blowing a soft kiss she turned her back on the grave, knowing it would be long before she could return.

"Goodbye." She mouthed into the air, sliding the necklace into her back pocket. Having stood over the silent grave Amelia took some comfort from having said goodbye the right way, though should 'goodbye' ever have been necessary with a life full of such prosperity, hope and happiness? Approaching footsteps came from June, her face red and puffy from crying.

"Hey ..." Amelia spoke comfortingly, her heart aching for the girl.

"She ... she's never coming back, Amelia, she's never coming back." June croaked.

"Maybe you're right Juney, but ... she's in our hearts. She'll always be." Amelia muttered.

"I don't want to say goodbye, I want my Mum back."

"Come here."

Amelia held her gently, stroking her fine brunette curls. Her niece was growing up, and so much like her mother. "She's gone baby, I'm sorry. It's hard, but we'll pull through together; we're tough aren't we?"

June laughed half-heartedly. "I'm not tough. Can I tell you something?"

"Yes, please tell me ..."

"I don't want to live anymore."

Amelia froze. June might as well have been reading her thoughts. She wasn't surprised, she'd seen it coming.

"Do you think your mum would have wanted you to say that?" She spoke harshly. *How can you say this, when you feel the same way.*

"No." June admitted.

Because she's my sister's daughter, she needs to be protected.

"Exactly, you can't think like that, June!" *How will you do it, will you jump or overdose?*

"Why not? What have I got to live for?" *I am not going to kill myself!*

"Yo ... you have me baby, I'm going to be beside you every step of the way, we're going to make it through this."

That's not what you're thinking though, isn't it?

"Really?"

No ... well, yes! I can't, I just can't live anymore. "I ... I promise!"

"Whatever happens?" June begged, sounding frightened. "Because she's gone."

"Whatever happens."

It was true, Emma was gone. Amelia felt the loss of love and her sister, all because of a bastard hiding in London. One day the killer would be hers. One day she'd exact vengeance on whoever had pulled the trigger.

Two weeks on …

A dazzling light shone through the partially open
window, reflecting off the leather-backed books on the
ancient wooden, carved shelves. Seated on a small
couch, she held a cup of cold tea, cupped in her shaking
hands. She held a tissue to her nose to stop the crying ...
stern instruction from Daniel Morse, executor of her
sister's will ... then added it to the growing pile at her
feet. Morse reached into his pocket and produced his
reading glasses. Amelia placed an arm around June's
shoulder. June sat crossed legged on the couch, head in
hands, crying silently; she was stiff from head to toe and
hadn't dared relax since arriving at Morse's office. He'd
been adamant he would not be making the trip to
Amelia's flat, ordering her instead to 'make the effort'
and come to his office. Today he was showcasing an
Armani suit, brown loafers, slicked black hair; the smell
of stale coffee swung on his breath. Amelia wondered
how long he'd stared into the mirror before work. She'd
come across him only once before, at a new year's eve
party. He'd shown her a friendly smile and they'd even
shared a dance. She'd despised him immediately.
Amelia hadn't known of the relationship between Morse
and her sister. Was he her lawyer? Friend? No … not
friend … the bastard had shown no sympathy. He hadn't
even shown himself at the funeral. Amelia stared out the
window. Right now she needed a distraction, anything to
stop the man from reading aloud her sister's
possessions. She felt she was violating Emma by
allowing someone to examine her things, yet it didn't
actually matter. Emma was dead, never coming back.
Morse sat forward.
"Thank you for coming down. I'd like to think you had
a safe journey?" He asked with a fake smile. Amelia

knew his concerns lay elsewhere – wrapping up as soon as possible.

"Journey was fine." Amelia replied.

"Now, you know why you're here?"

"Of course … the will."

"Yes, the will."

A few seconds of uncomfortable silence hung in the air while Morse irritably clicked away at his pen.

"So, you have the will?"

"Yes, I have it."

"So, shall we start?"

"Certainly." He nodded. His breath smelled. He placed his pen neatly back in his pocket, slowly leant down behind his desk and opened a second draw. Several long seconds of rummaging later he reappeared; a brown envelope in his hairy hand, its flap already lifted. Someone had tried to reseal it. She felt intuitively it was Morse's doing. Whether it was legal or not she couldn't be sure. When it all came down to the will it was certain that at some point he'd clapped his beady eyes on it, so why not now? He cleared his throat and lifted the thin envelope into the air. The will drifted from the envelope and, like a feather in the wind, floated down onto the desk. Amelia turned away. She couldn't bear to see it. Sensing her discomfort Morse snatched it up and bent forward. Without glancing up he began speaking sombrely, his words sending shivers down her spine. Even June had to straighten her posture.

"The last will and testimony of Emma Francine Gizzard."

§

"Don't let go." June mouthed in desperation, pointing to her Aunt's tight arm.

22

"I won't." Amelia's heart pounded with fear. "I will now read the will."

"The will, yes." Her voice croaked.

"I, Emma Francine Gizzard, an adult female presently living at Number 4, Albert Road, declare this to be my last will and testament. There may be changes made by myself or my representative upon my coming of age. I appoint Daniel Morse as executor of my will. I ask that he be spared court supervision and having to post a bond. If under any circumstance Daniel Morse is unable to fulfil his executorship of the will, then I appoint Amelia Alana Gizzard to replace him and to carry out my final wishes. I bequeath Number 4, Albert Road in entirety to June Gizzard, to whom I leave all my remaining property. I leave my partially cracked hand mirror to Amelia Alana Gizzard." Amelia's stomach churned with emotion, what was happening?

"I leave the remainder of my money to June Gizzard, to support her in building a life. Should any of my beneficiaries be unable to inherit as requested, I leave everything I own to my mother, Elnora Gizzard."

She was mentally so far away, so hung on her sisters wording that she didn't notice Morse waving Emma's signature in her face.

"Signed by your sister. I was there when she wrote it." Amelia jumped up from her seat as Morse produced the mirror. A fine marble handle, carved in great detail, an oval mirror with an oblique crack down its middle. It was beautiful, haunting … but what was its purpose, why had it been left to her? What was Emma's message? What was she trying to say?

"I don't understand." Amelia exclaimed.

"Why she left her property to her daughter?" Morse raised an eyebrow, too much emphasis on the word 'daughter'. "Wait a minute?" Amelia snapped back.

"You think I'm angry about Emma leaving her property to June? You think I'm jealous!" June stayed silent, chewing nervously on a thumb nail. Morse shrugged, surreptitiously slipping the will back into its envelope. "How dare you!"

"I would be upset if my sister left me a shitty mirror," replied Morse, a smug smile on his face.

"Maybe I'm upset she chose someone like you to read her will, you horrible little man!"

"Miss Gizzard, I do not consider this appropriate." Amelia laughed. "Oh, fuck off Morse, you're a liar and a cheat, everyone knows. Now if you don't mind ..." she nodded towards the will ... "I'll be taking my sister's document." Amelia reached over. Morse was too quick. He brandished the will high in the air.

"Sorry, can't do that Amelia, it would be illegal."

"And why so?"

"I am the executor of the will. I promised your sister I'd guard it with my life." Amelia was overcome with outrage. Why had Emma done such a thing, trusted this man with so much of her life?

"June, we're leaving." She sighed.

"I would be more than happy to escort you to the door," Morse offered. Pumped with fury Amelia turned on her heel, curved around the desk and gripped Morse's hands then snatched his glasses with one hand and flung them to the floor, placing a heavy foot on them until she heard a satisfying 'crunch'. Morse recoiled in horror, his face flushing from red to purple and back.

"I think..." putting her arm around June, struggling to contain her laughter, "we'll escort ourselves to the door."

§

"Did you see his face?" June howled with laughter, a generous bite gone from her vanilla ice cream.

"It wasn't something I was going to miss," Amelia replied, half-heartedly. The chattering of birds in the park was dying down, mothers were calling to children to come in for dinner. It was winter time and the sky was a soft violet; she guessed it to be around 5.00 p.m. Plenty of time.

"So, June," Amelia asked, "How are you feeling?"

June lowered her ice cream from her lips and swallowed the lump in her throat.

"What do you mean?"

"You have a flat, you have money. Your mother left you well cared for," Amelia said, kindly.

June shrugged. "Okay, I guess. But the flat, the money; nothing can replace her."

"I know."

June watched melted ice-cream trickle across her wrist. She didn't have the energy to stop it.

"It's hard." She whispered.

"I know."

"Do you?"

"Of course."

"Then how are you dealing with it so well?"

"Dealing with it so well? I'm only human June." In Amelia's ideal world she would have said 'Deal with it so well? You don't see me sneaking off to my room at all hours of the day crying until there's nothing left, I spend all day looking at photos of Emma. Or thinking about a logical reason for her death.'

"I know."

"I try and deal with it for you, June." June didn't reply, or attempt to stop her Aunt continuing. "You're so young, your whole life is ahead of you."

"So was hers, before they killed her." June hissed.
"You're right. But she would have died wanting her
little girl to live her own life, to stop grieving."
"I feel like I'll be grieving forever."
"You may never get over it, she was your mother. But
you'll become stronger." Amelia stopped and dipped her
ice-cream on June's nose. June giggled childishly.
"I mean we, will become stronger." She smiled softly.

§

The day was dim. Grey cloud low. Wind gushed
frantically; followed by heavy bursts of rain. City
workers rushed, shoved, pushed; cases and coats held
above heads against the weather. Amelia held onto the
bannister. The previous night she'd lain back exhausted.
Still, no sleep. Vivid images of her sister's coffin and
the will reading haunted her, memories too fresh to be
pushed aside. She knew it would be a long time before
she'd stop grieving. She wondered if June was coping as
well as she hoped. What would have happened if it was
her at June's age, to be told that her mother had been
shot? Would she have cried? Laughed?

§

Amelia tip-toed on the soft carpet, using the blue light
from June's digital clock to guide her down the narrow
hall. She felt mentally exhausted, abandoned. Shouldn't
her mother have been the one to deal with the funeral?
To have been first to hear the news? She entered the
room and immediately recognized her own trick; June
was feigning sleep.
"I think you should go to school today, it'll do you
good," Amelia said, sitting gently on the edge of the
bed, resting her hand lightly on June's back.

"Don't want to," June murmured; her face buried in her pink feather pillow.

"I'm going back to work today. I can't leave you here alone." She lied.

"You don't trust me?"

"Of course I do." Amelia sighed. "It's just … you need to pick up your life. It's your most important year in school and the longer you shut yourself away the harder it becomes to face the world again."

"You can't make me."

"Obviously not, come on. Do it, for me?" Amelia pleaded.

"No."

"Then do it for your mum."

"On one condition."

"Anything."

"Lay off a little; you're beginning to piss me off."

"Oh, right …"

"And one more thing."

"What?"

"This is for Mum, not you."

They sat in the kitchen; June slouched over the small marble table, Amelia glaring at the mounting pile of filthy dishes. An old radio hummed softly in the background. The tension was agonizing. She wanted to delve into the young girl's mind and shield her from whatever thoughts nested in her head.

"Want anything before school?" Amelia asked, busy with the dishes.

"No." She sounded bored.

"Some toast, anything?"

"No." She sounded agitated this time.

"Maybe we could go shopping later? You're always saying how you want a new bag?"

"I said no!"

Amelia leaned forward, a small smile creeping on her lips. "June, I know it's hard, to go back to school and face everyone. This is tough isn't it?"

"I don't want to talk about it."

"What's eating you June? Is it the house? Look, if it's that bad you can have another week off school."

"Just stop, please."

"Stop what?"

"Caring so much."

"Aren't I supposed to?"

"Not like this!"

"How do you mean?"

"You're acting like Mum never died, like everything's fine!" That hit a raw nerve in Amelia's mind.

"Look, darling, your mum is gone. I won't sugar coat it for you because I know how it feels."

"No, you don't."

"Trust me, I do. Maybe not fully, but I have a sense of what you're going through." And she did.

Amelia had once been a frightened soul, too scared to speak. Some nights she'd felt she should just run away, that she might as well have been dead. Some nights she'd lie in bed and dread waking up. Life was cruel, anxiety was all she felt. Little Amelia was a walking time bomb. So why had no one noticed? She'd convinced herself she was strong, like her mother, that her skin was a concrete wall. That she daren't worry. As long as no one could hear her thinking, no one could read her thoughts. What a mistake she'd made all those years ago...

"Whatever, I'm off."

"June." Amelia grabbed her wrist.

"What?"

"I'm here for you, you need to know that." Without a word June slammed the door, leaving a widening gap between herself and the woman who loved her most.

The woman whose love she was beginning to detest these days ... Amelia Gizzard. A distance that wasn't about to shorten.

§

The White manor.

Rokas White ran a comb through his dithering, blonde hair. God he hated ageing, even more he detested his vanity. He knew she'd be on the clock any minute now, he almost felt ashamed. The past can never be forgotten, he'd come to learn this over a series of painful years. What she'd driven him through, what he'd driven her through. She'd threatened to disclose his personality to the public ... the goddamn press. He smiled cheerfully at the thought of the press, unable to locate him in such a remote area, such petty people. Rokas knew full well what she'd been attracted to in the first place ... his wealth. Wealth that had come to him through 'Whites Trading Co'.
"Mirror, Mirror, on the wall, who's the greatest businessman of them all?" He admired his reflection.
"You, Sir White." A low voice replied.
His heart skipped a beat. In the mirror he could just make out her slim figure, framed in the doorway. He turned, embarrassed, and gazed at Katherine Marino. Stunning, so beautiful. Her emerald eyes watched his every move as he marched away from the mirror and sat at the narrow table. Despite her elegance something about her bugged him, made him feel edgy.
"Rokas, darling." She spoke softly, approaching the seat opposite him in the chilly room.
"Katherine." He spoke sternly, to make her feel what he'd felt all those years ago.
"Ro? Is it okay if I call you Ro?" She chuckled.
"Actu ..."

"So, Ro," she butted in, "you know, and I know there's been a little rivalry between us … no?"

He bit his lip. Well, had there been? He used every ounce of willpower to stop himself diving across the table and breaking her every last bone. She really could be nasty.

"Yes, I believe so."

"You see, my dear, I have a plan, a plan to put you back on top, a plan where you won't have to look in the mirror for confirmation of your business skills, but at the general public, who will adore you."

"Just tell me why you're here. I know you, Katherine. My guess is that you're not here to discuss … well, whatever you're gobbing on about."

She frowned. "Shame … we'd have made quite a team." She remained seated, adjusting her snug-fitting dress.

He hesitated. What if she was telling the truth? She could give him more; more power, more wealth. If she was right, who knew what they could accomplish.

"Okay, so, what's your plan?"

"I thought you'd never ask. It's ever so simple. This is a new age darling. Things have changed. Technology is at its height. Just think of it Ro ... Me, with my charm, you with your wit. We're more alike than you think. With our combined talents we'll be unstoppable. I want to change the way the world works."

"In what way?"

"Firstly, I want to eliminate all my enemies, people who pose a threat to my plans are your enemies also. Know the name Ryan Rain?"

"Sounds familiar…"

"I was doing a little research ... he's loaded, around ten million."

"What next?"

"My men are tracking him down as we speak, figuring out his daily routine."

"Then?"

"Then we strike, we become rich, we become famous."

"I … I think we should give it some …" Katherine cut him short. Rising from her chair she tossed a platinum card on the table and walked out.

There was a time his innocence had shielded him from reality; equally from his distant mother and secretive father. His mother had been poorly raised on the outskirts of Liverpool; his father, a wealthy businessman had used her to the point of pregnancy. That's when things took a turn for the worst. With pregnancy she'd been eligible for council housing then used her benefit money on her drug habit, expensive. In the process she wrote off her only son, they boy who needed her most … Rokas White.

Whilst his father supported another family, it was crucial that Rokas and Janice were kept a secret. That's when the blackmail started; Rokas was used as a go-between for hot cash. With this new money his mother's plans were not to move to a safer and welcoming community, not even to purchase a toy for little Rokas. In fact she envisioned something far different to what he'd expected. Boarding school. Rokas had fled boarding school to a life of crime and violence. Along came the business opportunities, no CV or qualifications needed, a turning point he couldn't refuse. Little did he know what he was in for. From then on life had gone downhill. Aged thirty he was involved in a ring of deception, drugs and murder. Then came the depression; no wife, no one to love. Every morning he'd open his eyes to another painful day. Mother and father refused to answer the phones. He was a burden on everything and he knew it. No lover, no child of his own. He didn't need children now; didn't need anyone to love. His parents had made sure of that. All he wished now was for his plans to grow into a major success. Revenge was an exotic aroma; he could taste it.

§

Years earlier.

The hospital was depressing, despite smelling clean, fresh, even welcoming. But underneath this people were dying. Amelia paced the hallway, past the coffee machine and bored eyes of the people in the waiting area, all around her were low conversations between patients and visitors. She was nearing her destination when her skipping abruptly stopped. She sighed in frustration and slowly turned back: she'd forgotten to get the coffee. Inserting a pound coin she watched the boiling water trickle into the cup; she knew she was using every means to distract her. She'd always had a fierce hatred of hospitals, but reminded herself that this case was different. She wasn't there to hold her grandmother's hand while she drifted off to dreamland, unaware her family even existed. She was there to witness the birth of a special little girl. Forty-eight hours of labour, screams and tantrums; a lot of blood too which, surprisingly, she didn't mind. The birth had required her to travel from university (she avoided re-turning home for Christmas and special occasions. Things were heating up in the Gizzard household). But none of that mattered, her niece had been safely delivered; pure, with exotic sea blue eyes. The account of her sister's pregnancy had been brief; she'd ended up having a one night stand with a man she didn't know, and still didn't.

Amelia walked through the ward with a real smile. Her parents were kneeling at Emma's side, engaged in a war to capture the special moment with their cameras. Emma sat closest to Elnora, staring down into her baby's face. "Thought of any names?" Amelia whispered to her sister, dabbing at the sweat running from her forehead. She set the coffee on the bedside table and threw her arms around Emma. The excitement in the room was palpable. Amelia contemplated the fact that she now had a niece; she settled on being ecstatic, with a hint of jealousy that could be pushed aside.

"I like ... June."

§

Present times.

"So, you don't like the colour?" June asked, holding the shower rose over her head.

"It's not that I don't like it ..." Amelia cringed at the purple water draining away.

"I knew you didn't like it!"

"Come on give me a break, purple's just not my colour." She laughed uninterestedly.

June rolled her eyes. "You said I could do it."

"Actually I didn't. You bought it without telling me, knowing you couldn't get a refund."

"I didn't know that I couldn't get a refund, anyway all my mates are doing it."

"Is this just some kid thing I'm not in on?"

"Don't call me a kid, I'm more mature than you think."

"You call turning into a big purple grape mature?"

"You see, you're not mature for saying that."

"Lighten up June." Amelia covered her nose from the sour smell of the hair dye. "By the way, that stinks!"

"Get out then?" June suggested.

"I'm already on it."

Amelia searched the cluttered fridge for the previous night's lasagne ... under a box of stale pizza. She unwrapped the dish and placed it in the oven to re-heat. Amelia thought about going to work early the next morning. Working in a supermarket wasn't anyone's 'thing'. Now that she had another mouth to feed, and getting more and more into debt with her university fees, she knew she had no other option. If she was to sacrifice her cosy little in- come she'd be jobless for a long time. Then what? The microwave beeped ... food done. She sliced the remaining lasagne into two portions along with a mixed salad. Setting June's plate aside she carried her own into her tiny living room and nestled into the couch, ready for her soap opera.

§

"I can't believe you fell asleep on me." June sighed, shaking Amelia's shoulder. Amelia's eyes shot open. She stared in disbelief at the untouched food beside her. She'd completely lost her appetite.
"What time is it?" She asked through a half stifled yawn.
"It's one in the morning." June laughed.
"Why didn't you wake me earlier?"
"You needed sleep."
Amelia's eyes examined June ... fully dressed, her cheeks a plush red, the night air still clinging to her clothes. Amelia shivered.
"June ..."
"Yeah?"
She was fully awake now. "You've been out?"
"Well, yeah, but I came in hours ago." June said nervously. "More like ten seconds ago."
Amelia leaned in closer.
"I can smell booze on your breath!"

34

"I might have had a drink or two." Amelia cringed.

"You're fourteen."

"I know."

"So, where did you go?"

"Just a friend's party, why … are you angry?" June asked cautiously.

"No, I'm not angry." She sighed.

A wide smile stretched across June's face. "Did you have a good time?"

"Yeah, it was good!"

"Good, I think you should head off to bed now kiddo."

"Sure." June stepped back and reached for the door knob.

"June?"

"Yeah?"

"Ask me next time, okay?"

June nodded her head, rolling her eyes. "Goodnight, Amelia."

"Goodnight, June."

It didn't take long for her eyes to shut again. That night she dreamt of a young girl flat out on the ground – clearly dead. An empty vodka bottle lying at her side.

§

Two months on …

June smiled happily at her reflection in the mirror as she ran the straighteners through her purple hair. Her uniform lay on the edge of the bed, untouched, still folded. School hadn't appealed to her today, in fact these days it never did. What was school worth anyway? It had been two months since she'd rinsed her mouth with vodka, spat it out, and sat in the garden for fifteen minutes. She was still feeling chuffed at having conned Amelia into believing she was drunk. Today she had a full schedule; a visit to the place she loved most. The place that only she knew of. Suddenly she scowled at the picture of herself and her aunt, pinned to the wall. It was all for show of course, but Amelia didn't know that. Amelia didn't know a lot of things. Has the very presence of another human being ever irritated you? These were the feelings she'd come to love and hate since the funeral. No matter what happened she knew she couldn't resist, would never find time to push them aside. It was the only way she knew to live. June thrived on searching for someone to blame, someone to hurt and transfer pressure onto ... Amelia Gizzard happened to be the perfect target. Amelia wasn't 'selected' as such. In her eyes Amelia had chosen herself. She was weak, nothing like the mother she'd known ... a strong spirited woman with an aura of steely attraction ... precisely what June saw when she stared into her bedroom mirror every morning. She knew she was strong, not so much physically as verbally. She'd been bullied once, a long time ago. Now she would be the bully, put them all to shame.

§

"June, dinner's ready!" Amelia called from downstairs. June clenched her fist at the sound of her Aunt's voice. She unplugged the straighteners and dashed downstairs. "I'm coming!" She hissed.

Amelia had disliked the idea of June 'going purple'. She was neither strict nor old fashioned, but well able to see disaster looming. She glanced at her niece several times, to make sure it wasn't a dream. How had she gone from teenage sweetheart to teenager-from-hell in such a short time?

Three months had dragged by since the funeral. She felt God was punishing her, that she'd been singled out for a pointless yet specific reason. People, friends, even distant relatives avoided contact. It was the awkwardness and pain of the situation that put distance between Amelia and life outside the brick walls of her London home. She needed to unscrew her head and dig out the painful memories. It wouldn't happen. Something else displeased her. For two successive weeks June had had her stomach pumped out ... a night on the piss ... she'd been forced to watch over her, laid out on the bed, tube's, sticking out from her young body making her look like an octopus. Life wasn't being reasonable. They sat watching television, the news blurring. June's attention lay elsewhere, Amelia's fixed on an event she could never have predicted, much less believe. She whispered three words over and over, like a stuck record.

"Rebecca Thorn: missing."

"Who's Rebecca?" June asked with sudden interest, interrupting her thoughts.

"Mm .. my best friend from university," Amelia muttered.

"When did you last contact her?"

"Before your mother died."

"What did you say to her? Why do you look so worried?"

"It's not what I said, it's what she said."

"Well?"

"It was a normal conversation, just a catch up, but then she began to sound worried. Before I hung up she told me to be careful ... of what? I said. But it was too late, she was gone."

"Did you always see her?"

"Not exactly, after uni she kind of avoided me. Why? I guess I'll never know."

"Sounds creepy."

"Poor girl, I hope they find her. I can only think of what her mother and father are going through ... lovely people."

"I don't get why you care," June said coldly.

"What do you mean?"

"You said she avoided you, so why do you care what happens to her?"

"Because I don't focus on the bad times, I focus on good times ... something you could learn from, June." Amelia replied, trying her best to hide the shock in her voice; did June know what she was saying? Then ... stony silence.

"I'm going out." June announced.

"It's a bit late!" Amelia protested.

"You're always trying to control me, aren't you?" June laughed, a frightening darkness in her eyes.

"What is it you girls do these days? Take drugs in the park? Drink till your stomachs cry bloody murder?" Amelia was fed up with her disobedience: the girl was only fourteen years old. Smart, but not street-wise.

"How dare you say that!"

"Because I was you once. You forget that don't you ... now are you going to sit the fuck down or walk out the door?" She almost winced. June paused momentarily, debating in her head. Take the advice or disobey? To sit was the easy option, to walk out the door was even easier.

What are you doing Juney, just walk out already. But she's trying to help me?

You don't need her help, anyway ... aren't you the one in control? "I'm going, there's nothing else to it."

"Your mum wouldn't have let you ... neither will I." Amelia sat back, her niece silently screaming for attention, ignoring her – it was the only way she could cope.

"Enough of this, I'm leaving!" June stood up.
"You walk out that door and I'm done with you, June. I mean it." She instantly regretted her words. June left the house, slamming the door with a heavy bang, leaving be- hind an uneasy auntie. But Amelia had already 'been there, done that', also once been young. She wondered how many adults lost touch with their inner child, ignoring the fact that they'd also once been youthful and rebellious. It had been different with Amelia and Emma, they were both stubborn, knew how to have a good time. The difference was … they'd supported one another despite their differences and an unstable family life; they knew when to stop. It would have been easy to fall into the depression and alcohol trap. But that wouldn't happen, except for June; she roamed the streets like the neighbourhood tart. It's what she believed she wanted to be, not what she really was. In truth, she was just a miserable child longing for a mother who would never return.

§

Emma was plainly a double for Amelia, with one small difference; Emma wore a great deal more puppy fat and had that slight 'sparkle' in her eye. Emma was the disobedient twin. No matter what havoc she caused, Amelia was dragged into it. Amelia had hated Emma's rebellious ways sometimes, could never understand her strange actions, but now she missed them so much.

§

Born and raised in England, Amelia lived in London in a petite 'eighties' style flat ... impossible to refurbish or re- paint. Her single couch was a boring black, her flaky wall- paper neither pattern nor design … just an unattractive lime green. Apart from that she adored the place; some- thing to call her own. She planned to keep it that way. It wasn't high rise, more like a mansion. She'd always wanted to live like her sister. It never happened. Her sister was brave, not afraid to take a risk. Emma was a gambler; not the card-playing type - she gambled with life, played life wildly, her family in constant fear for her safety. But her murder was inexplicable. No one in the family, or friends for that matter, could think of any enemies … or anyone at all for that matter … who hated her enough to kill her.

Amelia had not heard from her parents since the death; for that, she loathed them. But the time would come when she'd be able to forgive; she'd need to … for June's sake. They say time is a great healer, but would it heal her emotional wounds? Some days she felt dead, a lost soul, a hollow shell. Hours passed like minutes, work was over before she left the house. June was scarcely around, so it was like she wasn't there. She began crying for her sister, something now almost routine. Amelia felt like a drink but knew she couldn't; once she opened the vodka she wouldn't stop until she'd drunk every drop, then she'd become 'the octopus'. She couldn't allow that. All she could do was wait for June's return, then hold her hair back whilst she vomited and whined about life as a teenager. She just wanted her niece back, she wanted to stop the bad feelings eating her inside.

Seconds grew to minutes, and minutes expanded onto long hours. She knew she should have done more to stop her, forcefully if needed. Vivid images of June laying back in a stranger's car being molested by dirty older men whirled around in Amelia's head. June, dead, an empty bottle of Vodka by her side. June, helpless, with a broken leg. She became nauseous with worry … deciding, 'Sixty minutes tops'. If June didn't show up in that time she'd contact the emergency services. A small tap at the door soothed her worry ... Amelia sprang from the couch, ambled over to the door, drained, and unbolted it, latch by latch. Expecting a 'not so pretty' sight.

"Have you seen the time? I was about to call the police!" She began to raise her voice, and then paused in amazement. June was not drunk. In fact June was far from anything, like Amelia on one of her unbearable days – she appeared bored,

"Like … you give a damn about me. I figured you wouldn't care where I was. And no, I haven't been drinking, I didn't want to wake you 'cos you're normally asleep now."

"Not wake me? How was I 'sposed to sleep with you out all hours?" She realised then there was love somewhere between the two, a special bond, no matter how small.

"Look, I haven't been drinking. I don't see what your problem is."

"For God's sake June, have you any idea what I've been through? You know what … I'm not going to argue with you at this time of night. Just go to bed." Amelia hissed through clenched teeth, her eyes flashing.

"For months I've dealt with this, held your hair, not slept just so you wouldn't choke on your vomit. Help me June, please, so we can get through this together! You don't hate me ... you think you hate me. We're family, we share the same blood. I made a promise to your mother and that's a promise. I'm obliged to stick by you. I would never throw you away to a foster home and I certainly wouldn't abandon you, so let's forget this okay? Think of it as a yellow card! It's a chance we now have! A chance to start again and build trust." Amelia reached out with a mild smile longing for June to make some sort of contact. As expected, June declined, jerking away: Amelia's hand might as well have been lingering with a contagious disease.

"You can't tell me what to do." Amelia became furious, her temper worn thin by exhaustion. She closed in on June, breathing into her neck.

"Go … to … bed, and don't ever come in at this time again!"

"Fine!" As June pushed past her, Amelia noticed something and stopped her.

"Where's your necklace?"

"I lost it." June answered, staring at the floor; blatant lying.

"You lost it, the necklace, your mother's?" Amelia cried, followed by silence. The conversation was going nowhere.

"Just … get out of my sight."

Right there right then June made up her mind. She hated her Aunt. She'd never before hated anyone or anything in such a vicious way. Hatred … strong, pure … it could bring great things into her life. Her plans would succeed. She couldn't wait to reveal all, but for now she knew she'd have
to sit tight, be patient, play the innocent child. She'd fool them all.

§

The following weekend.

The beach was once a place for contentment and pleasure, a place where she and her mother could relax on the sand, listening to the pleasant sound of the tide drifting in and out. Then 'she' entered the picture, destroying the peace they'd carefully cultivated over the years. Life, the past few months, had been peaceful if full of corruption. June had enjoyed watching 'her' suffer, knowing the best was only yet to come. June sat up from the damp sand and watched three small children bursting with adrenaline, dash onto the sand – they were too far away to notice her, not that anyone did anyway. She took a deep drag on her cigarette, trying to order events in sequence. She gripped her temples and screamed silently. Her headaches were unbearable, she didn't know who she was anymore, she simply longed for her mother. She knew her life wasn't a life, but she didn't care. The beach was gloomy today, grey and cold. Unlike the times she'd been brought here by her mother. It was nice in a way, it numbed the pain. Sun meant happiness, and that would be silly, because happiness is not what she felt. Ever. A middle aged woman came into view from behind the children, observing their actions. June guessed her to be their mother. Mariana ran behind her children. She loved the beach in this sort of climate. It was fresh, sun only burnt her fragile skin. Suddenly she noticed a girl in the distance, a girl she recognized. June Gizzard. She wasn't particularly fond of Emma Gizzard, but realized just how vulnerable she was to being led astray, why would a teenage girl be alone on the beach on a day like this? It wasn't difficult to notice June's lack of interest in life, she needed a mother, someone to love. Poor girl.

"Be careful now guys!" She called behind her, watching June out the corner of her eye. Mariana's eyes suddenly widened in horror as a hooded figure approached June from behind. She began to sprint through the sand, unaware of her son swimming out in the tide, unaware that her children were nowhere to be seen.

June locked her lips around the rim of the vodka bottle, dribbling its contents across her tongue before letting it slide down her throat; it burnt. Her eyes rolled, her vision began to blur; before she knew it bile forced its way up through her throat, her hands locked around something steady, long hands, soft, comforting hands. "Hello June." Was the last thing she heard before being lifted off her feet.

The next day.

"You're sure?" Amelia asked, pressing the phone to her ear.
"I … I'm sure, Amelia!" Mariana said.
"So, you're saying you saw June, alone and drunk, approached by a strange man?"
"Exactly."
"So what did they do?"
"More like what did he do! She was being sick, she'd been drinking. He picked her up and walked away."
"You're kidding?"
"I'm not crazy!" Mariana screamed.
"I didn't say you were."
"My children are missing! That man, that horrible man! I know he took them!"
"Your kids will turn up, Mariana."
"They've been missing for two days ..." Mariana whispered.
"There's nothing I can do darling, I'm so sorry."
"She knows."
"What?"
"She knows, June." Mariana accused, fear in her voice.
"Mariana listen to what you're saying!"
"No, listen to what I'm saying." Amelia was silent.
"Your girl is a danger to herself, and a danger to those around her."
"I'm not going to listen to a forty year old woman accusing a fourteen year old girl of kidnapping her children, you're insane!"

"What would you do, if they were the ones you loved?"
Amelia was silent again, frightened to move. June
lingered upstairs, the second phone on loud speaker.
She'd heard the whole conversation. She smiled.
Goodbye, Mariana.
"No, I know she knows!"
"Please, leave my family alone!"
"Amelia ..."
Amelia pressed down the receiver and hurled the phone
across the room.
"June, get down here!"
"Coming," June said innocently.
""Now!" Amelia screeched.
"I see you like the beach!" She shouted when June's face
appeared from behind the door.
"Don't we all?"
"You twisted little girl. Do you also have a liking for
grown men, and vodka too?"
"What's that supposed to mean?"
"You know exactly what it means."
"Is there a problem?"
"Is there?" Amelia laughed. "Of course there is!"
"Well?"
"I'm doing my best here missy, why can't you see that.
Look at yourself. What in heaven's name have you
become?"
"What have I become? What have you become - more
like it!"
"If your mother could see you now she'd turn in her
grave!"
"You're wrong."
"Oh, really?"
"Yes, because it's your fault she's dead."
The first slap was overly gentle, but the next dealt the
full force of Amelia's anger. June stumbled two steps
back before falling to the floor. Her hand clasped her

mouth in disbelief. She stared at her auntie, her reddened cheeks and tearful eyes sending a rush of guilt through Amelia. But why?

"Oh, June, love. I'm sorry. We can work through this." She offered a hand. It was rejected as expected.
"Get away from me. I hate you. I hate you. I hate you!" June was up on her feet. She pounced rapidly, punching her aunt. Amelia seized her hair and threw her against the wall. June bounced back at her – ready to attack. Amelia had no choice but to retaliate. She ran at June, who dodged swiftly. Before she knew it she'd collided with the door, flat out. June raised her nails and dug them deep into Amelia's cheeks, she raked downwards creating five thin red lines on each side of her Aunt's face. Amelia came to with a scream. She instantly kneed June in the stomach and threw her back. June rolled and came to a stop at the door. As Amelia climbed to her feet she felt pain surging through her temple, June's foot sent her rolling onto her back once more. She could smell copper, blood.
"Where are they?" She panted, holding the side of her head.
"Piss off." June spat in her face.
"The kids, what did you do?" She cried with horror. June laughed stiffly. Amelia glared. Hiding her fear; too bruised to move. She heard June's steps around the kitchen. She couldn't help but close her eyes. A few minutes later she sensed June's presence and opened her eyes. Her jaw dropped; heart stopping fear tightened around her chest, her eyes bulged. A shiny blade in June's white knuckled hand glimmered under the hall light.
"What's wrong with you? Please, June, listen to me, this isn't going to solve anything. Just put the knife down. I can help you. We can go and see someone, a shrink,

anybody." Amelia reached delicately for June's wrist, ready to die if she had to. This could go two ways, or they would both be escape unharmed if Amelia could charm her way out.

"Get up." June ordered, wrapping Amelia's hair around her fingers and throwing her onto the stairs.

"Do you know what it's like living with a pest?" June laughed.

"No."

"I do!" She screamed.

"I'm sorry if I'm a pest, it's only because I love you!"

"I'm supposed to believe that?"

"It's true."

June shook her head, a smug smile on her face.

"Are you going to hurt me, June?" Amelia pressed.

"I'm not going to hurt you." Amelia sighed with relief.

"I'm going to ruin your life."

"What?"

"Get off me!" June suddenly let out an ear-splitting shriek. Amelia jumped back. What now?

"June, what are yo ..?"

"Get off me!" Again she let out a shriek. "June, I'm not tou ..."

"Somebody, get her off me." Surely her cries of distress must have been heard several doors away. Amelia gingerly manoeuvred herself off the stairs and stepped away from her. June twirled the blade, slicing away strands of her hair. Next, she slashed her face. Blood streamed from the wound. She neither flinched nor cried. Yet still the screams came. She hurled herself into the wall, wounds from their earlier fight aggravated by her self-harming.

"Put - the – knife - down, June, put - the - knife -down." Amelia begged, horror perching in her system. June tilted her head and gazed at her auntie, blood dripping from her cheek, loose hair clenched in her hands. A

47

bloody smile fixed on her face. "You did this to me, Auntie Amelia." She lifted the knife high into the air.
"Don't do it!" Amelia cried with desperation.
"Why not?"
"You have things to live for, you've got me, grandma, grandpa … I'm begging you!"
"Oh, please. I'm a wreck but I'm not going to kill myself." She smiled.
"What?" Amelia looked at June, clearly deranged - totally perplexed.
"I'm going to enjoy seeing your rotten ass in jail." The words 'ruin your life' boomed in her head.
"June. No!" June wasn't bluffing. She'd finally snapped. Maybe something dormant since she was a tiny girl, maybe something bitter at the death of her mother. The niece she'd come to love and care for was gone. Why? Amelia had failed her sister and hated herself for it. She stood transfixed. June thrust the knife deep into her abdomen, just left of her stomach and slid lifelessly to the cold floor, she had said what was not able to be put into words.

Amelia was certain June would survive. The police would arrive sooner or later. But she had to flee; leave the London area. Had this been June's strategy all along? Her ears pricked at the distant scream of sirens. Why so quickly? Oh, dear God she needed time. Amelia clasped her hand to her chest, she would think later. Shock. Disbelief. It was now or never. She could remain seated and attempt to explain why a teenager lay flat out in front of her, a knife handle visible in her gut. Or she could do what she always did ... run. For if she stayed, June could claim a vicious victory.

§

Reality

The first few rings she'd ignored through ignorance; thinking of the outside world frightened her, people watched behind her back, judging her over Emma's murder and how she'd distanced herself from her family. Sadly, after the fifth voice message things took an unwelcome turn.

"Elnora Gizzard? This is Amanda McIsaac, homicide detective at …"

"I know who you are, you said so in your messages," Elnora snapped.

"Good. Do you know why I'm calling?" Amanda asked patiently.

"Look, I told you all I know, please just …" She had become tired and uninterested in questions about Emma, they were all too alike, and all un-answerable.

"This is not about Emma, Mrs Gizzard."

"What is it about then?"

"It's about your granddaughter, June Gizzard." Elnora's hands trembled.

"What about her?"

"There's been an incident." Amanda stated.

"What sort of incident?" Elnora asked cautiously.

"Miss Gizzard, I can't sugar coat this for you, we're treating it as an attempted murder."

"Treating what as an attempted murder?" She cried out.

"The attack on your granddaughter." Elnora's mouth opened but no words came out. Her little June, attacked? She tried telling herself that the word 'attempted' meant she was still breathing … it didn't work.

"You must be wrong, where's Amelia?"

"We don't know."

"I'll give her a call and tell her to drop by, she must be distraught."

"Miss Gizzard … I'm afraid that won't be possible."

"And why not?"

"Because, she ran ..."

"Ran?"

"Yes, she's nowhere to be found at present."

The sudden realization began worming its way into her stomach, she felt sick.

"Don't you dare!"

"I'm sorry?"

"Don't you dare put this on her head, I know an accusation when I hear one!"

"Who else could it be, Miss Gizzard?"

"There has to be some sort of mistake?" Elnora pleaded, almost 'begging', praying that Amanda was mistaken, that there was a computer fault, anything else.

"There's no mistake Miss Gizzard. We're certain. Your daughter assaulted June."

"How certain?"

"Certain enough."

"How do you mean, certain enough?"

"I don't think I'm in a position to say …"

"Oh, it's always the same with you people, petty games." She said icily.

"This is not fun and games, I assure you."

"Then tell me what you think?" She was getting angry.

"We think Amelia may be implicated in your daughter's murder."

"How involved?"

"We think she pulled the trigger." Silence.

§

Amelia's life was on hold. Looking back, she knew everything could have been over in seconds. She'd run like never before, her legs taking her who knew where. She was outraged, distraught, and fast losing her sanity.

She'd hunkered down in some back alley … no idea where … amongst trash cans and litter. Not the nicest disguise, but sort of incognito. Her mind spiralled out of control. What next? Was this it?

What had been an hour had passed like seconds, it was wrong, out of control. One thing was certain; June had played the vengeance game very effectively, but why? Why such violence on herself ... cruelty to the people who loved her most? There should have been someone she could have turned to? Sooner or later her parents would read or hear the news. What she needed was her mother's soft voice, to be told that everything would be just fine. Her recent detestation of her mother had subsided, leaving behind child-like desperation. Hands shaking she raised her mobile skywards and squinted her eyes through the fogginess of the alley, a bar of signal showed visible on the screen. She struggled to dial numbers she thought she'd long forgotten. After several rings she heard it.
"Hello?"
"Mm … Mum?" Her voice trembled.
"Amelia?" The voice chimed.
"I need you to know that whatever has happened, it was not my fau … "
"Listen!" The voice became intense. Threatening.
"Don't call me!"
Amelia bit her lower lip. "Mum?"
"You can't call me. If they find out you've contacted me I'll be in big trouble. You're all over the news." She now understood the hatred inside her, why she'd detested her mother all these years. She'd never quite accepted the distance between herself and her mother. She recalled the many occasions she'd all but begged for compassion, only to be pushed away.

"Mum, stop it, you're scaring me!" She began to cry stifled tears.

"Stop crying." Elnora demanded. She stopped, muffling her sobs.

"What do I do, Mum? I swear, I never touched her. I wouldn't lay a finger on her."

"I don't know what to think. If you get caught you'll be arrested for attempted murder." What shocked her most was that her mother believed she was capable of killing at all ... and not just anybody ... her own niece.

"Amelia?"

"I'm here."

"I have to go."

"But m ..."

Silence ...

Was this how things would always be? Amelia's green eyes filled with tears. Her cramped hideaway gave her backache but she didn't want to leave its safety just yet. There was only one person left she could turn to. She dialled a different number this time.

"Yello." The strong reply didn't alarm her. Dad always sounded different on the phone.

"Dad?"

"A ... Amelia, is that you?" He whispered.

"Yes, Dad, It's me!" She cried, and then cursed herself for the loudness of her voice, one wrong move could easily expose her.

"What's going on Amelia?"

"I don't know, I really don't know."

"Right, you need to be calm ... calm."

"Calm, yes."

"Amelia?"

"I'm here Dad, I'm here."

"I know it wasn't you." His comforting tone calmed her racing pulse; same old Dad. Tears came to her eyes once more. So, he'd seen all the lies but had not taken fool to their influences. Her old man wasn't as bad as people said he was. As bad as she thought he was.

"I love you, Dad." She sniffled.

"I know it wasn't you, Amelia, I'm your Dad, for crying out loud. I know a killer when I see one." Amelia shivered at his words. She didn't ask when it was he'd last seen one, now was certainly not the time to pop that sort of question.

"Dad, could I co …"

"Of course you can. You're my flesh and blood. I'd rather die than let the police take you."

"I don't know how to get to you." She said, suddenly panicked.

"I'll come get you, where are you?" Amelia told him. He described to her a place they both knew, not too far away.

"I'll be there in 20."

"Thanks, Dad … love you."

"You too." He replied simply. She trusted him. He wouldn't let her down. Throughout her life he'd made many mistakes, but now she envied him.

§

She smiled uncomfortably at the bloodshot eyes staring at her across the table, deep rings below them, black and blue. June twisted her hair in her hands making no attempt to dry her tears.

"I'm a mess," she said dryly.

"You look pretty," replied Amanda. June rolled her eyes and sat forward, crossing her arms to cover the stab wound. "Sit back, June, relax."

"I'm fine like this, thank you."

"Fair enough." Amanda shrugged. "You do know why you're here?"

"Of course, you're going to ask me ..." She straightened up and pointed at her stomach, "about this."

"Yes, that wound."

"Well, go ahead."

"What time did you arrive home?"

"Around 3 a.m."

"And then what happened?" Amanda was mindful not to upset the girl.

"I went into the living room and smiled at her; she was sitting there ripping up pictures of my mum," June whispered, barely audible.

"Do you have any idea why?" Amanda pressed.

"No, all I know is she's hated me ever since the death."

"Why?"

"I don't know."

"Is it because of your drinking?"

"What?"

"You're drinking, you drink don't you?"

"Who told you this?"

"The hospital."

"I might have got drunk with some friends, like maybe two times."

"Not so long back you were admitted for a stomach pump, weren't you?"

"Why are y ..?"

"Weren't you?" Amanda repeated, arching an eyebrow.

"Y... yes."

"Why do you drink, June?"

"Because I need something to urm, to..."

"To numb the pain?"

"Yes." She said, grabbing at Amanda's words.

"Obviously she shouldn't hate you for drinking, but we'll determine that later. Carry on, please."

"What do you want to know?" "Everything from where you left off."

"Well, naturally, I asked what she was doing. She snapped at me, I started crying and snapped back. She stood up and my heart dropped; if you could have seen the anger in her eyes you'd have bolted. She walked up to me and shoved the pieces from the pictures in my face."

"And then you hit her?" Amanda asked boldly.

"What? No, of course not!"

"Right."

June exhaled and continued. "Then she told me to stop crying, but I just couldn't stop. That's when she hit me."

"And you hit her back?"

"No!" June growled.

"I was only asking, sweetie."

"You're making it sound like I did something to provoke her."

"Did you?"

"No, I didn't."

"Were you drunk at the time?"

"No."

"We'll be asking the hospital if there were any traces of alcohol in your system."

"What's the point, I've told you the truth?"

"Just a precaution, I'm sure you understand?" She smiled.

"Whatever."

"Carry on, please."

"Yeah, so she hit me."

"And?"

"She hit me again."

"What did you do?"

"I froze. I didn't know what to do, couldn't speak or scream. I just let her hit me, throw me against the walls, tear out my ..." She held up a loose strand of her ruined hair.

"But the neighbours said they could hear screaming?"
June narrowed her eyes. "That was her."
"Did you run?"
"Yes, when I thought she was finished ... I ran to the
door. It was locked. When I turned to see where she was
she ..." Amanda didn't need an answer. She studied the
wound carefully, all the while a voice in her head
screaming, 'Self-inflicted'.
"You telling me the truth?"
"Yes, I swear on my mother's grave!"
"Give me a moment, sweetie." Amanda left the room,
her stomach doing somersaults.

§

"I'm telling you, Charles, something isn't right." She
spoke softly, keeping an eye on June - on the other side
of the glass - staring into space with dead eyes.
"After all your years in the business, I'd say this is one
of the easiest cases we've ever had:

'Manda. Physco Auntie murders sister, attempts to finish
off dead sister's daughter – the niece - and to top it off,
she runs.'

"It's not rocket science ... look at that girl ... she's a
wreck ... outside and inside!"
"But Charles ..."
"There are no buts Amanda. It's case closed until we
find this Amelia girl. I want choppers, search parties.
Find her!"
he hissed.
"You can be a real bitch sometimes, you know that?"
"Yes."
"Good. Get back in there and sort that girl out."

"Where'm I going to live?" asked June as Amanda entered the room.

"You'll stay with us for now ... protection." Amanda wanted to reach over and shake her... root out the truth. "Any idea where your auntie would be?"

"Probably in bed with a man; she was the neighbourhood bike." June laughed bitterly.

Amanda's jaw dropped.

§

Cherry Cottage

Her crooked lips formed a wide 'o' and stretched back as she yawned, blinking the sleep from eyes that felt like they should shut and never open again. Amelia's eyes followed the ray of sun that had managed to sneak in through the dust covered window. It lit up the faded pink paint on the bedroom walls. She ran a finger across her bedside table. Grey powder clung to her skin. She shook her head with disgust and wiped her hands on her robe. More dust ... the room hadn't been cleaned in years. She rolled over and clambered to her feet; she had to get out the room before she choked. She tried the light switch and rolled her eyes, it didn't work. She knew she was procrastinating, because she'd have to face her father, face the memories, face the previous day's horrific 'incident'.

Amelia leaned against the door, she didn't care about ruining her robe ... probably wouldn't wear it again, and allowed herself a moment to compose herself. She couldn't delay any longer so taking a deep breath she wrapped her fingers around the door knob and turned it. "Dad?" She rasped loudly, stepping out the door to lean over the staircase. She didn't bother looking around the house for memories, she'd been too worn out the night before; still felt that way.

"Dad?" She shouted again, surveying the first level of the house. Empty, like the air inside it. What was going on? Where was he?

The house had once been her haven, full of pleasant memories, out of the London area, set amongst rows of crops and grass, her personal artificial countryside. Now, the crops were dead. A dark shadow hung over the property; where the brawls had taken place. She and Emma would crawl out of bed and find their parents arguing, mostly over their marriage. Then came real fights and ornament throwing. Holding her pet cat in silence, she'd listen carefully. Hours later she'd be full of regret and anger. Despair! Divorce soon followed. No more family outings, no more picnics or good times. Growing up happened far too quickly. The twins became a problem for their distraught father. With a mother who'd never called, and a father who'd never listened Amelia assumed that life would always be like that. But then she broke free, went to university ... but dropped out. She and her sister travelled the country desperately seeking help. Once, Amelia had got a job waitressing and become stable enough to afford a small flat in the city centre. She'd also hunted desperately for someone to love. A year later, and her sister was murdered. From then on, her life turned for the worse.

§

She looked in the dirty kitchen in search of something to ease her dry throat. Throwing away sour milk and mouldy juice she settled on a glass of water; it tasted funny but she was too thirsty to notice. She found some cereal in the fridge, strange. She wouldn't be able to eat it, not even with milk. She chewed the flakes carefully, undecided on whether or not they were past their due date. Frowning, she inspected the small rounded table at which she sat; no flowers in the vase. The house had once been more 'feminine' than intended. Elnora had seen to that, and it had angered her father deeply. But why? Had she done it purposely, to be awkward? Or was the man generally nasty about everything? Now, all signs that a woman had once lived here were gone. The walls were coated a gloomy navy colour, no framed pictures, just walls in an empty house sheltering a hollow man. That's when she began to worry; she was concerned for her father. To think that this was it, his daily life ... nothing more. It was a life he was wasting; sad to see, especially since Emma's death.

Things were strangely silent, not quite right, until her father stumbled in the door, his pants stained with oil. "Morning, honey," he greeted cheerfully. His mind, though, somewhere else.
"Hi, Dad." She replied, forcing down more dry cereal. He paused momentarily.
"I'm going back to the garage, project," he announced. What where these projects that swallowed him whole? Cody had rotted in that rust bunker for days on end in the past, slaving away at some secret pleasure.
"Dad."
"What is it?"
"We need to talk," She said grimly.
"Not right now, darling," he replied, politely yet dismissively.
"Can't you look at me when you're talking, Dad?"
"Of course." He sighed in frustration, turning to face her. She noticed the bags beneath his eyes.
"What's happening to you?"
"I'm perfectly fine."

"I'm worried."

"Don't worry, the police won't come here."

"No, I'm not worried about that; I don't care about the police. I'm worried about you!"

"Why?" He leaned forward, oblivious to what she was saying.

"What's happening to you?" She repeated. "The house, it's so plain."

"You're not worried about being a fugitive, you're worried about the décor?" He giggled.

"You're not listening!"

"Okay, I'm sorry. It's perfectly natural for you to worry about your old man, but really, I'm perfectly fine."

"You're not; this is wrong. We don't talk anymore, me, you and Mum … everyone's drifted, yet you both seem perfectly content with that. It's all so wrong. Ever since the divorce, the death, nothing seems right. I can't go on living like this anymore, Dad! Have you looked outside, the way you're living?" Slowly her tears appeared.

"Oh." She hiccupped.

"What's wrong?"

"I get it now!" She cried.

"What?"

"It's my fault. I never visited, I never made the effort."

"Oh no, no, no!" He protested, kneeling down on one knee.

"Yes, you know it's true."

"None of this is your fault."

"Tell me, Dad?"

"Tell you what?"

"What this is?" She sighed.

"This is an old man who's too lazy to clean, don't you worry about me!"

"No, Dad, this isn't just you and your cleaning skills, this is the whole family, me, you, Mum, June."

"June ... that girl." He growled.

"I know, but we have to think of the reason behind it. Who knows what she was thinking?"

"I know," he agreed.

"Back to us." She said, not wanting to be steered off topic. "You're not okay, Dad, you're falling apart. One day it's going to be too much."

"I will never fall apart while I have you and Emma."

"Emma's gone, Dad."

He hesitated. "She's ... still in our hearts."

"I guess you're right."

"It's okay, come here." He drew her into a fatherly hug.

"Do you think about it?" She whispered, her head resting on his chest.

"About what?" He stroked her hair.

"Emma ..?"

"Not a day goes by when I don't think about it, but life must go on. I promise you, this will be over one day, and you won't have to run or hide."

"What if I want to run, want to hide?"

"Well, you just have to be strong, you have to face it."

"Face it. How?"

"One step at a time, they can't harm you if you can't harm yourself." Then she had a dramatic gut feeling that she wasn't just running or hiding from the police ... there was someone else along the line, something completely out of the equation.

§

Two days later.

Amelia's eyes fluttered open effortlessly, a complete change from waking up with a throat clogged with dust. The air was filled with the burning scent of bleach, it was incredible how much she'd scrubbed the previous two days to improve her father's living conditions. She sat up and had a sudden urge for comfort, for her elderly cat that had returned. She'd recognized Smudge instantly.

She jogged from the room, happily throwing open every window in her path to let in the fresh breeze; she had a thing for cold air. She went into the living room, aware that despite knowing she'd have to leave soon, the place was healing her; reminding her of the few good times. Her nose suddenly scrunched up and she stopped. No more bleach smell! She recognized the all too familiar smell that always trailed behind her, death.

Her cat lay in a bloody puddle on the floor. A furry mess, splattered across the carpet, a large brick by its side. She stumbled back, frightened. Smudge … how long had he lain like this? This was no accident, it was callous killing. Someone had been in the house ... she shivered. Could whoever had killed Smudge also be on her trail? Her heartbeat accelerated; this couldn't be happening? It wasn't fair. It was never fair. All she wanted was one night free of killing, a little time to rebuild her self-esteem and plan her life, more time to heal.

Snapping out of shock she rushed to the kitchen and seized the sharpest knife she could find, picked up the phone then stamped on it in a rage ... she couldn't even phone the police!
"Dad!" She screamed through the kitchen window, like a small girl again, afraid and needing parental affection.
"Coming, Petal." Her father burst into the room.
"Follow me!" she cried, grabbing him by the wrist and leading the way. Cody Gizzard stopped dead in his tracks the minute he saw the cat, the hairs on the back of his neck rose. Smudge had been part of his life for nine years. He wrapped his arm around her waist protectively

and took the knife from her; readying for an attack. He signalled silence. Once sure they were safe for the moment he released his grip and let the knife fall to the floor.

"Bastards."

"Oh, Dad." He moved away, ignoring her affection. "When I catch whoever did this, I'll break every bone in their body." It was rare for Amelia to hear her father react this way, with hate. But why shouldn't he be mad? Amelia shared his rage; she just had an unusual way of expressing it. Why would someone kill a helpless animal? She imagined the scene in her mind ... Smudge, being slaughtered whilst she and her father were either in or out the house. What she couldn't figure out was ... who was it? The same person who'd killed Emma? No, that's silly. Someone knew their location. Amelia suspected she was

no longer safe, that her little safe haven had now been opened to the rest of the cruel world. She also realised she had let her stupidity get the better of her, of course her father's house would be the first place someone would search in order to find her? That very same person who had entered the house could go to the police at any moment. She needed to leave, but much to her discomfort had resolved to stay the night for her father; it couldn't do any harm ... could it? She'd break the news to him the next day.

She stood, one foot on the frosty grass, watching her father bury the cat. The house was bringing back too many precious memories; memories she couldn't face right now. As she laid in bed that night questions haunted her. Why her? That was the main question. What if her mother was in danger? Would she be putting her mother in more danger by visiting her? Around 3 a.m. she managed to drift off into a grey sleep.

§

"Have you been up all night?" She asked. They munched on marmalade toast and scurried through the morning paper.

"No." A lie.

Amelia sighed, adjusting her dressing gown. "Talk to me, Dad."

"About, what?" His head lifted reluctantly.

"Stop bottling it. You're sad about Smudge and still grieving for Emma, I can see it."

"That's the problem with you Amelia, you interfere too much." Amelia was taken aback. Did she really interfere too much … or even at all?

"I'm trying to help."

"Leave it!" He snarled.

"Fine ... by the way, I'm leaving tonight."

He dropped his toast. "Wh … what? Where will you go?"

"Don't know, but the longer I'm with you the more danger we're both in." She sat beside him; he stared mindlessly into space; it worried her. Like yesterday, the talk they'd shared seemed never to have happened. He averted his gaze to the photo of the twins.

"It seems so strange without her. What with us being twins and all, I guess it makes things worse."

"Try to forget."

"Dad, you gotta realise I'm a fugitive now." She shed a few tears, the usual. "I'm scared, I'm scared a police officer will come to the door at any moment, especially after what's happened to Smudge? What are you doing about that, Dad. Someone knows how to get in and out of your house?"

"Shhh." He pulled her closer, cradling her once more. For a few moments they huddled in silence. A pin could be heard dropping in the room. Then, as though it had been perfectly planned, her unspoken fear happened; the door burst open. She looked at her father in a panic. One thought ran through her head as she dived to the floor ... 'This is the end.'

§

When danger looms a person undergoes an instant mental or physical change of state as adrenaline kicks in, ready for whatever threat lies ahead. Sixty seconds remained before she'd be located; either by the police or by the unknown killer there to finish the job. Her father's silent gestures screamed 'hide'. A strange mental force paralysed her. She was too terrified to flee yet at the same time not wanting abandon her father. The refusal to flee was too strong. She'd stay, face up to whoever may enter. The door creaked open. She held her breath. Three suited men, armed with heavy weaponry, entered the room.

"What do you want?" Her father asked protectively.

"Let me introduce myself." The tallest man stepped forward, he had a raspy tone. "I have been sent by R. White. I believe there is unfinished business between the pair of you."

"Dad, what is this?" Amelia interposed.

"Be quiet," the man commanded.

"Excuse me?"

"Do you want to share the same fate as your sister?" Amelia's eyes widened, a cold shiver flashed down her back.

"You, it was you ... wasn't it?"

"I'm sorry?"

"You." She stepped forward. "You killed my sister ..."

The man laughed. "Stupid girl."

"You bastard!" She screamed, launching herself at him, beating his chest. He threw her back at her father without effort.

"Control her, Cody."

"Why aren't you doing anything? He killed your daughter!" Amelia shrieked. Cody hung his head, unable to look at either of them.

"Tell your boss I haven't got it, but I'm working on it," he muttered.

"I'm afraid that won't happen." The man raised his gun.

"Let's not do anything silly now," Cody whispered, slinging a shielding arm around Amelia and then backing up in an attempt to put distance between him and the man. The man followed his foot-steps, shadowing him with his huge frame.

"This is from the boss."

§

Amelia lay in the corner. She felt dead, yet weirdly, alive. Her hands shook nervously. She was alive! If she had lived then something was wrong. She opened her eyes.

"Am ... Amelia, come here."

"Don't die, oh God, I'm begging you, Dad." Amelia tugged at her hair; furious at herself. Cody had taken the bullet, to save her.

"I need to tell you ..." hand held to his heart, struggling for breath.

"Tell me what, Dad, tell me what?"

"I ... I'm sorry baby, me and your mum we ... we're no ..." He coughed, the life seeping out of him as each second went by.

"Not what, Dad, not what?"

"We're not your birth parents."

Her face turned chalky, her hearing became muffled, she felt dizzy. All these years, her whole life ... her 'mother' and 'father' had been strangers to her. Her birth parents could be 'out there'.

"They'll be after you now." He slurred.

"What?" She snapped back to the present.

"Those men, you must hide."

"What've you done?" She held him close.

"I'm sorry baby, it was for the best."

"What are you talking about?"

"Go, hide. They killed Emma. They're after you now; you know too much. Go!" A violent cough racked his body. He was gone. Amelia held him in her arms, the tears came. What was he trying to tell her, 'They'll be after you now?' What had he done? The killers and Cody had known. They could have had their asses behind bars, but it was too late now.

Amelia was alone in the world now; no one to comfort her, she couldn't even turn to the police. Her birth mother and father could be out there somewhere, anywhere, and she couldn't search for them because she was now, according to BBC news, a psychopath. The police would doubtlessly visit soon. She knew she should feel shock as the news her father had sprung on her, but wasn't it just another thing to throw on the pile? She wiped her tears on her sleeve. Nothing was right. The lone life was a life she wasn't ready to live. With no family, no friends, she'd never be content. She once thought 'normal' was over-rated, but now? What about her sister? What about the dead man who wasn't her father? Who ... was R white?

§

It had been long … too long a day. Amanda could only dream of nightfall, then the hours would be over. Alone, she poured a generous glass of wine, before raising it into the air.

"Happy birthday to me," she chirped gleefully to herself, only then to bow her head in sadness. The house still remained an empty shell, no relatives or friends or welcoming glow, just her. She felt too tense to feel emotional right now, instead she knocked back more bargain wine. It was supposed to be 'her' day, instead she'd fallen for the emptiness around her. She was too tipsy to acknowledge the constant hammering at the door; the ringing of the bell.

"Why are you here, this is meant to be my day off." She spoke stubbornly, her fuzzy mind reliving memories of deceit, times of compassion and love.

Charles's glance transferred to the empty bottle staining the cream carpeting.

"You're drunk. That your first?"

"I repeat, my day off."

"Not any more. Grab your coat."

"And why's that?"

"I'll explain on the way, you need to see this …"

§

She'd run again. She was a good distance from the house, unsure whether or not the police had arrived, hoping Cody's body was in good hands; not lying face down in a ditch or ripped apart and scattered over the countryside. She had willed her legs to work, at the same time trying to sort the files in her mind into order. Hopeless. In the end, knowing the police were not far off had forced her to focus on one goal … getting as far away as possible. She'd finally doubled up in pain and fatigue, bewildered at the location to which her legs had carried her.

She inspected her accommodation; not much really, a bedroom, kitchen and en-suite. Clean but smelling slightly of mothballs and rotting wallpaper. For the moment it would do. Meantime she'd have to gather her thoughts. Amelia rested on the raggedy maroon couch against the wall in the bedroom, shuffling awkwardly to avoid loose springs.

Judgement time. What was really going on? First, Emma is murdered; then Amanda McIsaac breaks her promise of 'keeping in touch'. June cracks, succumbing to her hatred of Amelia, claiming Amelia was the root cause of Emma's tragedy. In time, June's schizophrenic, or bipolar, or just plain crazy self unravels. She repeatedly beats herself and conjures up sob stories of some sort for the police, leaving Amelia helplessly on the run, later to seek refuge from her mother 'Elnora', only to be rejected and forced to contact her father. Who was now dead.

The fact she'd been adopted was a blow; she was still taken aback, numb with disbelief. Her family had no more right to be called a family. How would Cody's death affect the old woman? Amelia was simply not immoral enough to ignore his death. It pained her to accept it, but the reason her life was in jeopardy had rested in his hands. Yet he'd taken the bullet for her. If not for him she'd be a corpse, most likely under a light on a metal table, her body being dissected. She acknowledged him for that; tears began burning her eyes. Why so much weeping? So much shit in so little time? At times she'd felt her life had ended the moment her twin had died. So, what was really happening in this whirlpool mess? It didn't feel as though a piece of the puzzle was missing, more like there was no puzzle at all. No logic. All she knew was that since Emma's death everyone and everything had spiralled out of control. Somewhere along the line Cody had messed up, big time. Exhaustion soon kicked in. She felt drained, as though through a colander. Time to rest. Surely the police wouldn't stake out this rotten dump?

§

The sun reflected off the freshwater stream, mirroring its surroundings.

"Daddy, it's beautiful," the little girl called.

"Isn't it just, sweetie?"

"Can we get ice cream after this, Daddy?"

"Anything for my little girl." The man stared mindlessly into space only half attending to his daughter. He felt rotten; because of his actions his daughter's life would become a hellhole. It felt to him like raising a pig for slaughter.

"Look ... baby, I need you to know something," he whispered.

"What is it, tell me, Daddy?" The cheeky grin, desperate for an answer.

"I've done something bad, lied and cheated many people."

"But why, Daddy?" She began crying. "You always tell me never to lie to people; why would you do that?"

Passers-by watched the little girl sobbing.

"Calm down, I'm sorry, okay, I am so sorry, but you need to know everything right now, right here to prepare you for life. Okay, here it goes!" He breathed in, massaging his wrinkly temples.

"I ..." He was interrupted by his wife approaching.

70

"Why is Mummy here; isn't this our special time?" The little girl shouted after him. He left her standing at the water's edge. When he returned he said, "I'm so sorry petal, I know this was meant to be our day but Daddy has to go to work. I'll take you to Mummy's, okay?" She said nothing; she couldn't face him. He was a liar. He'd betrayed her. Where was the daddy she'd once loved and admired?

"Let's not mention this to your sister, okay?"

"You know what, Daddy?" She turned and faced him, cheeks red with anger.

"What, sweetie, come on, I'm in a rush?"

"You make me sick!" She twisted away from him. Amelia's eyes shot open, tears staining her face. She found it difficult to breathe as the realization struck home ... she was that little girl.

§

The female glared into the apologetic eyes of the adolescent standing in front of her, sucking on her Lambert and Butler, its filter covered in red lipstick.

"You really are letting me down!" Her voice was calm, but with an edge to it which hinted she might 'blow' any moment.

"I'm sorry, I just ... it's hard!" She slapped her.

"You idiot, get out there and kill her ... do something!" She grabbed her by the scruff, and whispered in her ear, "Make her suffer."

§

What time was it? How long had she slept? Amelia felt lifeless, frail and shaky…what was that dream? A figment of imagination, or a corrupt memory? It was unquestionably Cody, of that she was certain. And that bawling little girl was definitely her. But why the confession; what work? He'd been about to reveal everything to her at that moment, but something had frightened him. Something was wrong, and it seemed impossible to figure out. And why wake up in tears? Why had the dream hurt her so much?

Besides the dream and several other nightmares she'd ignored the fact that she was dangerously hungry. Normally she'd nip out to the shops, maybe flash a quick smile at the locals. Normally she'd snuggle under the duvet and watch television whilst sipping a lukewarm tea. Normal didn't to exist in her world any longer. She wasn't cut out for this type of life, not strong enough. Ridden with self-doubt. Her fear was walking in the open, being recognised and taken on the spot, either by police or the men of R-White. To change her appearance was one thing, but to change identity was a different matter. It would have to be done if she could ever again walk freely in public. Ten minutes on and she still sat in front her reflection in the split mirror leaning up against the grotty tiles in the repulsive bathroom. In her left hand rested an old rusty carving knife. In the other hand half a tube of black hair dye she'd rescued from under the maroon couch.
"Here goes nothing…"

§

Cherry Cottage.

"What's up with him?" Amanda pointed to a uniformed man leaning head down, heaving into a wheelie bin. "One of the new recruits. Poor guy's never attended a murder scene before," Ron replied sympathetically. "Detectives, he's inside. The team have collected any evidence possible, fingerprints. But if there's more, let me know. I'll be in touch soon," A man from the forensics team said. They shook hands.

"So, it's a he?" Amanda asked as she slipped into her white overall.

"Someone's an eager beaver." Ron teased.

"No, not an eager beaver." She lowered her tone before turning to face him. "This someone is right ticked off. My one day off, Ron, my one day off."

"It didn't look like you were doing much." He retorted.

"And what's that supposed to mean?"

"Go get some coffee; I can smell the booze from here."

"So? I had a drink. It's my birthday!"

"Do you always drink on your own?"

"I'm new to the city."

"Oh, boo hoo."

"That doesn't change what you put me through," she mumbled.

"Oh, here we go … I do remember you were the one who ended it?"

"What do you expect? You hopped into bed with my cousin!" She hissed.

"Just get to work." He ordered, blushing.

"That's right, brush it under the carpet like you've always done."

"You sound like my mother."

"Except I'm not your mother, I'm the girl whose life you wrecked."

"State the obvious?"

"I thought you said get to work?"

"Go on then."

§

The Duke's Arm.

Her once golden curls had now become a short, thin
greasy mess. Her clothes where creased and stained.
Who was she? What had she become? She couldn't hide
here forever. She'd rather be shot; it seemed preferable
to rotting in a dump like this. Her main concern was
food; where to obtain it. Her growling stomach
reminded her that dying of starvation is not uncommon.
Without a thought she was off, skulking through the
same gaping window through which she'd come, careful
not to dislodge any remaining glass. She hopped off,
landing on the smelly bins then leaped down onto the
ground. Cautiously she made her way through alleyways
leading to the pub. She'd certainly chosen a private area;
no one should suspect too quickly. Amelia breathed in.
This was it … her time to find out how the world would
respond to her.

§

A rose can represent many things: love, passion, hatred.
Emma was the first to begin her voyage through life;
toddling at age one and speaking at age one-and-a-half.
"What this, Mummy?" Her wide, chunky jade eyes
twinkled.
"It's a rose."
"Can I pick it?" Babies, infants, call them what you will,
energetic beings bursting with life and love. Yet they
know nothing of the world into which they may be
dragged. Emma was one of those children.
"No darling, you need special gloves for that."
"But Mummy." She clasped her tiny fingers into a
pleading position.
"Oh, go on, just pick the top." She tapped the child's
nose affectionately. Emma bent down on her knees. It

was a showery day, not unusual where they lived.
Gently she prised the top of the rose from its stem. Cold
water trickled down the petals onto her chubby arm; a
strange yet pleasant feeling. She giggled. Raising the red
rose to her nose she sniffed.

"Mummy! It's lovely!"

"Isn't it, petal. Come on, let's go and pick up Amelia."
She smiled, amused at how the infant responded to the
rose.

"Okay. Can I take it with me?

"Sure."

They began walking. Emma stopped suddenly.

"Mummy?"

"Yes?"

"Rose is my favourite!"

§

Holding her right hand in her left, she walked the streets
of London. Except, she couldn't stop, wasn't physically
able to open her eyes until ...

"Oh, love, I'm sorry!" A sweet voice stroked her ears as
she lay on the cold concrete. Slowly she lifted her
eyelids. A heart-warming sight, a woman no older than
sixty. The woman flicked her long red hair, visibly
losing its vibrant colour to a battle against old age.
"Silly me, here let me help you up." She extended a
wrinkled hand. Amelia took the hand gratefully. It was
the first normal contact she'd had since Cody had been
shot. She studied the woman carefully. *Has she
recognized me? I bet she thinks I'm a killer! I need to
get out of here, now!*
She commanded herself to speak. "I ... I'm sorry, it was
my fault." Amelia laughed. The woman's eyes tilted as

her heart began to feel sympathy for the girl in slept-in clothes and in need of a good scrub. Homeless no doubt.
"No, it was my fault. Here let me make it up to you."
"It's fine."
"Come on, you look like you could use a good brew."
"Well, I'm in no rush."

§

The bungalow was too big to be considered a cottage, yet too small to be considered a house. It reminded her of something from a fairy-tale. As they entered through the terrace the woman reached for her hand, causing Amelia to enter stealth mode.
"Don't be scared…"
"Why, shouldn't I be?"
"I'm trying to be nice to you."
Amelia Sighed. "I'm sorry; I guess I'm just not used to it."
"Used to what?"
"Trusting anyone, it's kind of what I believe in."
"Then why did you come here?"
"I guess, well … I … I guess I trust you."
"That's good."
"I suppose."
"My name's Deborah, Deborah Fane. Most people call me Deb."
"Nice to meet you Deb, my name's ..."
Your name? Think!
"My name's Emma."
"No second name?"
"I wouldn't want to say it, it's foreign and tough to pronounce."
"Well, nice to meet you Emma. Come along I'll put the kettle on!" The living room was all she'd ever dreamt of. The scent of cinnamon drifted by. Although the lights were dim, several pink candles were placed at

each corner of the room. The walls were a sunny green shade, the carpet a whirlpool of snowy white - a type that makes you take off your shoes and walk bare-footed.

"So, what's your story Emma?" Deb passed over a steaming mug, and settled a plate of biscuits on the coffee table.

"I don't have a story," she replied, her head locked down into the mug, letting the hot steam brush her nose.

"Everyone has a story."

"Not me."

"Oh, come on!"

"Very well, my mum and dad hate me. I'm not wanted."

But you are wanted, your face is all over the news and the papers.

"That doesn't sound good."

"Look, can we cut the bullshit? Why did you really invite me here?"

Deborah's face became tense. Amelia wished she'd never opened her mouth.

"You look homeless, like you've been through a lot." she said defensively.

"You could say that." Amelia whispered.

"Hey, life sucks. But you know what? You're sitting here feeling sorry for yourself. You want the good things in life right? Every good thing counts and you should make the most of it. But you're not getting any of the good stuff while you're here. So finish your tea, and get off your ass!" Deborah was kind, and vulnerable, someone Amelia didn't want to drag into her unsolved 'issues'.

"You're right. I'm sorry if you hoped for a long chat."

"Oh, I'm sure I'll cope, Good luck Emma I hope you succeed."

"Thank you Deb."

"Come back, won't you?"

"I promise." And she would. The offer of a cup of tea and a quick chat was rare these days. She liked Deborah, a lot. It was a light walk, then a sturdy pace. Before she knew it she was sprinting back into the city. Then she realised she couldn't just sit and wait for rescue. She'd have to seek out the truths, forgotten so long ago. She'd need some form of contact with her mother.

§

It was a cold night. She had no coat, no hat, no gloves. Nothing to warm her body. She stood, hunched. The telephone box was far from the city centre. The air was still, not a face in sight. Stepping over piss and grime she managed to punch in the dreaded numbers after inserting a fifty pence piece she had scavenged from the floor.

 "Hello." It was a relief to hear a soothing tone. But there was always a bombshell to come, which saddened her. "Mum, I need you!"

"Oh, Amelia I can ..."

"Mum, please, I'm begging you, I feel so alone."

Not even her warm tears could warm her cheeks, or her heart.

"My husband's dead." An appalling silence hung at the end of the line.

"What's that supposed to mean, do you think it's my fault Cody is gone?"

"Dad." She slowly realised the mistake she'd made.

"Amelia, what do you mean, Cody?" Her mother's tone became serious.

"Just come and meet me, I'm be ..."

"I will go nowhere until you tell me why you called your father Cody!"

Amelia paused, speechless.

"Amelia!"

"Okay, okay. I'll tell you!"

"What is it then?" Elnora pushed.

Her grip tightened around the phone, more tears trickled. Truth time.

"I know the truth."

Distressed screams heard at the end of the line, why, who, what?

"Mum, talk to me?" she cried.

"I'm so sorry; it's not your fault."

"What do you mean?"

"Just, I need to go."

"Stop, just stop!" she screamed. All my life, lies, lies. Why, Mother, why?" The screams grew louder.

"Calm down, love, please, I can't deal with this, not now!"

"So what, you'll just shut me out, your so-called daughter? Tell me, Elnora, just tell me, how did Cody die?" Her cheeks sizzled, red with stress and anger.

"Don't call me Elnora, don't you dare! I raised you from a baby; I am your mother whether you think it or not. It's not my fault, it's his! I tried to protect you; he had a heart attack, for Christ' sake!"

"You lying bitch. He was shot! You know everything. Tell me the truth!" The screams were deadly at this point. She knew she'd struck luck for no one to notice her break down, but she didn't care. All she knew was that Elnora had been stripped of dignity.

"How do you know he was shot?"

"I was there!"

"What?"

"He took the bullet for me! Something you, so-called mother, would never do. You make me sick!"

"Why are you doing this to me?" Elnora moaned.

"Because you both screwed up my life. What happened all those years ago? What where you getting into? Just tell me!"

79

"I ... I can't..."
"Why not?" she pleaded.
"It would destroy you. Your father he ... was messed up."
"What?"
"I have to go Amelia, I love you, I'm so sorry for everything, I hope one day we can be a family again."
"Don't you dare," she demanded. "Don't run away from this, not now, tell me the truth!"
"I ... I, I'm sorry."

Nothing, just the annoying buzz of a dead line. Amelia hurled the phone at the wall and watched it swing back and forth. Back and forth, just what her life felt like; constantly back and forth to the past, back and forth for answers she was afraid may not be there. She began her walk back, slipping her hands in her pockets and biting the string hanging loose from the top of her hooded jacket. Little did she know there were eyes on her back; that she was being watched; every minute of every day. Every minute of every night. Ever since the day she was born.

§

Katherine Marino fiddled with the miniature umbrella gently bobbing from the rim of her green cocktail, the background humming soothing sounds of Sunday radio.

'And that was Counting Crows with, Colour-blind.' The DJs voice floated to and from her ears. 'Mum and Dad thought I was crazy. Wow did I prove them wrong. I love my job! I love playing music for my people. Now I know we're all itching for some forecasts so over to Martin for a quick weather update.'

'Right folks, get outside whilst you can, because today seems the hottest we've had in a good while. Slightly over forty degrees. Have a great day guys - over to you Dean.'
'Well, you heard him, get outside! Up next ... Toto … Africa.'

Katherine shifted her focus from the radio to once again to look at 'it' ... a fountain, standing tall and proud outside the sliding doors to her beach home … a limestone block carved in the finest detail. Its design showed a child wearing a crown, a pair of heavy angel wings on its back. It reminded her never to forget the time a masked man had beaten her, costing her life's precious miracle, her unborn child. It had been a straightforward message, but on whose instruction? The beating had been brutal, the side effects calamitous. She'd never have a family.

Katherine turned away from the fountain and allowed her robe to fall to the marble floor, fully aware of her beauty. She slid into the crystal blue pool, the welcome sun warming her body, the only heat she'd felt in a long time. She was grateful, pleased she'd made a life for herself.

There had been two 'formal meetings' between her and Rokas the past couple of months. The restaurant had come as a disaster; he'd done a runner, left her to wait and nibble on over-priced bread. He'd called a day later; they always did. 'They' meant all the stupid bastards drawn into the world of 'wealth' and 'charm' they're promised, the so- called world of Katherine Marino. Her riches had come one day after she'd dropped out of high-school and begun lounging with her aunt and uncle; her father hadn't wanted a failure in the house.

Then she became acknowledged, soon becoming the face of modelling magazines countrywide. No longer 'Kate' she was now 'Katherine' an icon with a fortune, and a real kicker when it came to being a lawyer. She could hurt people with words; able to win people over with one short sentence. She could do anything. But, alas, she was human, and a human can only take so much. When she lost her baby it was the end of the road, no more modelling, no more defending people in the courts. She was now doing the dirty business, ratting on criminals and hiring bounty hunters for anyone standing in her path to glory. She failed to accept that she herself was a criminal, a spiteful, grudge-bearing monster and now it was too late to turn back happier times when she'd been loved.

Rokas was due to arrive in about ten minutes. She planned on using her stunning appearance and attitude for the pair of them to embark on some sort of mission, mostly to boost her ego. She'd decided on finishing with Ryan Rain. She didn't need his money, didn't need to kill him; she just wanted someone to bear the pain she'd endured. She'd get what she wanted in a short while, for the moment she'd wait. Swimming under the water she vaguely made out a figure standing over the edge of the pool. Surfacing, she recognised the figure as Rokas.
"You're early." She pronounced rudely, annoyed at his arrival.
"Hi to you too."
"Let me just … slip into something."
"Oh, I'll go and wait somewhere else?"
"It's fine; just keep your eyes closed." He turned away. Then he turned back around, astonished at the slowness of her movements, at her golden skin glistening in the sun. She was stunning. Shame it would all soon go to waste.

"Am I gorgeous?" She teased, throwing herself into Egyptian cotton.

"Well, urm …"

"Take a seat!" She ordered, pointing to a sun chair.

"Urm, sure thanks."

"Now." She settled into one of the chairs. "Oh, wait, would you like a drink or anything?"

"No, thanks." He smiled.

"Right, let's talk business."

"I want to get to know you, Katherine."

"Go ahead."

"Drinks miss?" A man in a bow tie interrupted, steadying a selection of cocktails jiggling uneasily on a silver tray.

She looked down at her empty glass.

"Pina colada please, Michael." The drink was put in front of her.

"Sorry, do continue." She said, returning to the conversation. He leaned in.

"How many people have you had killed?"

"Well, three, maybe four. Does it matter? Do you think it makes me tough? You think I'm indestructible because I know how to hire a bounty hunter?" She twiddled her hair, sipping her piña colada.

"No, but I think that's what you think."

"Look, just get to the point," She barked. He massaged his forehead

"I need to tell you a few things." He said slowly.

"Go ahead?"

"You know this Ryan Rain guy?

"Yes."

"Well, his real name is, rather, was … Cody Gizzard."

§

83

"When you say 'was', it better not be a joke." Katherine raised an eyebrow.

"Don't worry, I had him sorted."

"And the money?"

"I'm working on it."

"I presume I get a cut?" she added.

"And why is that?" Rokas said in confusion.

"Well, you wouldn't want the law involved would you?"

"Katherine …"

"You're a smart man, Rokas. You beat me to it and no doubt the money should be yours, but that doesn't bother me because I get what I want, understand." She smiled scornfully.

"There's a problem; his daughter is a fugitive."

"How is that a problem?"

"Once she returns home, the money from the will is hers. She knows nothing of her family's wealth and I want it to stay that way."

"I can sort her out." Another sip of colada graced her mouth.

"No, I don't want her harmed; just diverted."

"Why ever not? Kill her and it's all good."

"No, it will ruin everything." He muttered sternly.

"How's that?"

"Some special plans."

"Can I know?"

"Certainly not. In fact, I don't want you in this." Rokas shook his head.

"Well, I want my money."

"Okay, Jeez, twenty percent if you keep quiet and leave the girl?"

"Forty." Katherine demanded.

"You're a bitch Katherine, but whatever." He lied effortlessly; she'd get nothing but what she deserved. They shook hands.

"Rokas?"

"What is it? I gotta go."

"If you killed the other Gizzard girl, why are you keeping this one alive?" she asked, wearily.

"What you talking about?"

"You killed her father, surely it was you who killed her sister, I've read all about it."

"That's just it ..."

"What?"

"I didn't kill the Gizzard girl. I don't know who did ..." He left her breathless, confused that a third party was now involved, but who? Did she really know Rokas like she thought she did, what was he crafting under his criminal hands? Then he was gone, never to return. Never needing to return. Because only he knew that these were Katherine Marino's last minutes. She could live her fancy lifestyle, cheat the courts, avoid jail time, and even have someone killed at the click of her fingers. But, at the end of the day ... she couldn't cheat death.

§

In the past.

A distressed man cradles two new-borns in his arms. To his right sits a stocky man in a glossy suit; the suited man is pressuring him, causing the babies to cry.

"I ... I can't, oh God, just give me more time?" The man on the left pleads, a desperate attempt to calm the screaming infants. He punches the flowery wall. His head is spinning.

"They are mine! It's them or the money!" His eyes fixed on the man in front of him.

"I can ..." He is interrupted. The babies suddenly stop crying; silence fills the room. The two men turn their heads towards the disturbance. The wife of the man on the left stands, stiff, shaking, glaring to and fro from her babies to the man on the right.

"Don't you dare touch them!" she warns, her veins pulsing through her neck. She's deeply disturbed.
"What are you going to do, lady?" The man laughs.
"Sod you!"
Slowly she withdraws a pointed object from her sleeve; a chef's knife. She points it at the man in the suit, shaking, attempting to show no sign of fear, but not thinking straight. The man knows this but is still taken aback.
"Put the knife down." He laughs.
"Don't tell me what to do!" she shouts, closing in on him.
"Whoa, steady lady." He beings to feel threatened; does she really mean business?
"Get out of my house!" she cries, waving the knife about.
"Okay, okay, calm it!" He raises his hands defensively. Eventually he leaves, the loud bang of the door restarting the crying. He'll be back. She drops the knife and herself to the floor; fainted. She lies still on the floor. The lookalike babies shriek like never before.

§

Amelia felt nothing but rage and betrayal. She frowned at herself in the mirror, felt sick of everything. Her whole life was a shamble, a lie. She might as well have never been conceived. Most of all she wondered about her birth parents. What were they doing now? Were they thinking of her? If only she could meet them, share her side of the story, discover what had really happened all those years ago. She felt imprisoned in a world in which corruption followed her. She needed answers! But how? Would the fact of Elnora's contribution make her crack? Or would the demented woman reveal the truth? Only Amelia could decide. After all, she'd put every last ounce of her faith in the woman, but ... care for her anymore? Elnora wasn't blood, but ... she had raised her, from a very young age.

She was glad to see no clocks hanging from the walls, time in the pub seemed to pass by fast, considering she wasn't living a life. She forced her eyes to stay open despite knowing the one thing she needed was a long sleep to conserve energy. She was in for a bumpy ride. Sleep came easily that night, her dream bank offering a strange variety. In one dream June and Emma walked off into the sunset. Amelia tried running but an invisible force restrained her,
holding her motionless on the ground. She screamed silence. She reached out, begging for her sister. Her sister offered no help of any sort. June's lips formed an evil grin as she took her mother by the hand and led her away from Amelia, helplessly fixed to the sand, sinking slowly.

Amelia awoke in tears, that was certainly a new one. She'd grown to detest these horrific 'nightmares'; wished they'd leave her head for good. She yawned, scratching her ratty hair, needing a shower.
Unfortunately not possible at the moment. The world outside was sunlit, an offer she couldn't refuse. She rose sluggishly from the couch, slipping on her trainers. She'd taken the precaution of resting in her clothes; no one would want their bare skin touching a couch like that. She casually, but finally, managed to sneak out through the ruined window. Taking her usual route she hopped out into the street. This time people stared, but not at the fact she was a fugitive – rather, at her dirty appearance.

§

"I'm sorry miss, we don't allow the homeless." The old woman sat behind a wooden desk blocking off the rear end of library, whispering every word.

"I ... I'm not homeless," she argued, feeling slightly insulted, but knowing deep down it was, sadly, true. Amelia's hide-out could certainly never be considered 'home'.

"I'm sorry, I just assumed."

"You prejudged." Amelia corrected.

"Look, I don't mean to be like that but it's policy."

"Why do you think I'm homeless?" she snapped.

"I don't like to speak where I shouldn't ..."

"Go ahead."

"Okay, well you're rather dirty. And you smell the opposite from what I would consider nice."

"Look." Amelia leant forward, ignoring the comment. "I have an address."

The woman sighed. "I'll look it up on the engine, what is it?"

"14 Elder State Lane, my name's Elnora Gizzard." The woman stopped abruptly.

"Elnora! Oh my lord, it's you!"

"It's you!" Amelia squinted and focussed on the nametag pinned neatly to the woman's knitted top - 'Judith'.

"Forgive me for being so rude, gosh, you look so young."

"Same to you."

"I heard about little Em, why ... such a tragedy. That night I prayed two whole hours for your family, and then it came to me that little Amelia got into a bit of bother, have they found her yet?"

"Nope, still looking." Amelia chewed on her upper lip, wanting to re-direct the conversation. How long would it be before Judith identified her true identity?

"Okay, so what can I do for you?"

"I'm looking to use the computers?"
"Well here's a tag with your username and password, in case you forget it." Amelia's eyes followed the words.

User: El68
Pass: JuneGizzard

"It was great seeing you Elnora, I'm sorry about before."
"Forget it; it was nice seeing you too." Choosing the computer at the back, Amelia finally slumped into a swivel chair, wondering. Keeping a watchful eye she peered across to Judith, seemingly distracted by a man claiming to be delivering a selection of 'K.R' Novels, she wondered if Judith was sane. Hitting the 'home' button, Amelia began typing away. Her first search produced a variety of results; some useful, some not. Again she refreshed her search ... 'R White.'
A list of names and numbers filled the screen. 'White, Ryan. White, Ricky …"
Once more her fingers were busy at the keyboard. Narrowing down her near impossible search to, 'R White, London.' That's when the miracle occurred.

§

Newspaper clippings, 1989-1995. WHITES WONDERS

'Dragged up in boarding school may ruin a child, but not Sir Rokas White. Yesterday morning a wealthy Rokas offered a donation of £270,000 to several charities dotted across England, quoted as saying, "I shouldn't have the money, I don't want the money. I'm helping people… for that I'm happy."'

MARINO AND WHITE BATTLE

'Rokas White, charity giver. Wealthy business man. Katherine Marino, stunning model, fantastic lawyer. Both loved by the nation. But who will win the nation back? Yesterday saw Mr White held up in the crown court, as Katherine Marino continued with her allegations of white being "A murderer and a criminal". Further investigations will continue. Anyone with information is urged to contact the number below.'

"Interesting…" Amelia whispered to herself. Her focus completely gone from Judith who was silently approaching her. Amelia massaged her temple, frustrated. No concrete evidence of 'R White' being a criminal seemed to come to her. She resumed reading …then in an instant, she wished she'd turned away. The sight of the last clipping was to tear her world even further; churn her insides like butter. It read: WHITE LIES: HE TOOK MY BABIES.

In the past ...
The woman rests in the rocking chair, cradling a baby in each arm. She sings tenderly to them, hoping they'll soon settle. Her husband stands in the doorway, his face filled with fear for his wife's wellbeing.
"Want me to take over?" He asks softly. She doesn't answer, instead she stares at him with pure hatred; hatred that increases daily. The bags under her eyes reveal extreme tiredness but she'll never abandon her children into the arms of this monster.
"You need rest," he pleads, gently placing a hand on her shoulder.
"Get away from us." She roars like a female protecting her cubs, rejecting his affection. He sickens her.
"Don't do this."
"Don't you dare put the blame on me!" She begins crying; she stares at her new-borns, so young and full of life.

"This isn't my fault, it's what you want!"

"It's for our own good, please, believe me!"

"You were about to let him take our children!" She screams.

"I don't think you realize the danger of the situation. It has to be done."

"Get out of my sight you bastard, you will not give away our children, we made a commitment!" She spits at him in disgust.

"Technically, they're not ours …" The woman suddenly slams her foot down, the chair stops rocking and the babies begin screaming. She stands up and lays them down.

"Not ours?"

"Well, we adopted them!" She slaps him.

"You horrible little man, get out of here. How can I love you now?" She shouts at him. He settles down, silently, refusing to leave.

"You think I wanted adopted children, why can't I have babies?" She continues. He covers his face.

"Answer me!"

"I thought so …" She shakes her head. "Your so-called friend forced a knife into my stomach, didn't he, took away my chances of having a family. Do you know how that feels?"

"Stop it!" He roars.

"Exactly, now get out. You deserve nothing, you selfish piece of rubbish!"

"Please ..." He begs.

"I said go!" she screams, cuffing him. She wants her natural body back, but it's too late. She must help children that aren't hers make their way in the world, away from this man. She smacks him once more. He retaliates, knocking her to the floor. Looking up, her face is a mixture of blood and tears.

"I'm taking them away; you're never seeing us again. I will do whatever it takes to protect the twins."

"No, don't do this." She shakes her head, unable look him in the eye. Will she ever?

"If that man comes back, I'll kill him," she warns.

"Come on, get up." He reaches out but she rejects him once again. Slowly she heaves herself up. She's dressed in her work clothes, of medium height, someone who could be considered a natural gem. She rips off her silver plated name tag. It glides across the floor and under an antique bookshelf. Six bold letters are engraved on it, six bold letters these babies will come to love, and hate ... Elnora.

§

"Er ... excuse me." A stern female voice drifted into her ears. Amelia closed her eyes, hoping for a guardian angel to reach down and whisk her away, tell her it was all lies, that she hadn't been kidnapped, that it was her birth mother's choice to give her up to a pair of complete strangers.

"Amelia!" The voice grew louder. A dozen heads shot up, as if hearing the name 'Amelia' was the signal of a celebrity. She kept her eyes on the ground.

"I know ..." The voice was now a soft whisper. "You're not Elnora."

"Judith?" Amelia finally spoke, her eyes still glued to the ground.

"You should stay where you are."

"Why?"

"Because the police are on their way."

Amelia placed one heel behind the other, ignoring the eager audience of pedestrians waiting for her arrest. Positioning herself carefully she aimed her full bodily force at the exit sign, imagining the word 'exit' really represented 'freedom'.

"Don't think about it; just imagine what you're putting your mother through?" Judith said in disgust.

"You have no right to say that." Amelia hissed.

"And why not?"

"Because she's not my mother!" She shot from her seat. She knew her chance to talk would come in the future. Behind her trailed shouts and remarks, insults. Her ears were a force-field to anything that happened or could be heard in her surroundings. She sprinted through the park, avoiding dogs and cyclists and a group of local runners. When the sirens began, she knew it was time to pick up her pace. She'd walked here once before, when things had

been right, alongside a toddling Emma and a happy mother. When things had once been right. Then there was a collision, not so brutal; more of a time waster.

"Hey, watch it." Amelia bawled, raising a hand to the blood running down her forehead.

"It ... it's you!" Amelia blinked several times, the figure that had knocked her down stood, back to the sun, generating a glowing rim around its body. But even through blurred vision and a fuzzy mind, she knew the figure only too well.

"Elnora ..." She gasped.

§

In a computer-lit room, around a table fit for a small army sat four detectives, each involved with the Gizzard case. Each wanting answers ... each wanting the day to finally end.

"The girl knows more, I'm telling you Sam!" Amanda cried.

"Please, keep your voice down." Sam replied, gesturing with a hand.

"Give her a chance," interrupted Harley.

"Just carry on Amanda," Charles quickly put in, to prevent Sam dishing out more orders.

"I was talking to her when she first came in; she spoke as though she hated her auntie. There were always reports of June being drunk, taking drugs. As much as it looks like Amelia is to be blamed, I think the girl is playing a part."

"That's obscure; a teenage girl causing this much mayhem. Are you suggesting she killed her mother now, then killed Cody Gizzard along the way?" Sam shrieked, followed by harsh, chesty laughter.

"No, Sir. I'm not saying she killed her mother, or grandfather."

"So, who do you think killed them?"

"Not sure yet, but to go by the look on your face I have a feeling you think it was Amelia Gizzard."

"I have a right to suspect." He retorted.

"Of course you do, Sir, but trust me … Amelia Gizzard is not a killer."

§

Shock amplified in her body, heavy rain frizzed her short messy hair. How long had she sat motionless on the ground?

"Amelia, speak to me!" Elnora pleaded through the strident storm. A spark of lightning flickered, followed by a roaring thunderclap. Amelia looked to her right – suddenly her worst nightmare had come to physical form. Standing at the gates stood the same men who'd gunned down her artificial father, presenting a barrier with their large piggish bodies. Terror moulding her face she quickly glanced left.

94

"Amelia Gizzard, you are ordered to remain where you are." A voice echoed through speakers in the hands of a policeman. It was not a pretty sight; three riot vans parked perfectly behind four police cars. They stood together in the centre of the spotlight. The helicopter was doing a repeated circle. No chance of escape, she knew that.

"Are those the people, who killed him?" Elnora whispered. She didn't reply.

"I'm sorry, Amelia."

"If only you meant it," she said bitterly.

"I mean it, I am."

"This isn't the time or place for apologies; you can talk to my sorry ass when it's in jail."

"That won't happen, because you're innocent."

"So, now you think I'm innocent?"

"I don't think, I know."

"You don't mean that." Amelia stated bluntly.

"Amelia … I want you to listen very carefully to me." Again she didn't reply.

"Amelia, do you trust me?"

"I don't know."

"Well, you need to, because times running short!"

"I ... I can't."

"Do you trust me; do you want to get away from here alive?" Silence.

"Amelia!"

"Okay. I trust you." Amelia sighed, she was tired of it all, she just wanted rest. Elnora put a wrinkled hand into her Gucci handbag, but what she took out was totally unexpected. Amelia staggered backwards. Elnora caught her, then twisted her arm very slowly. Her wrinkled hand moved ever so slightly and Amelia's eyed widened in horror at the touch of a cold object against her neck.

"What are you doing?"

"I told you to trust me, Amelia."

"Then get the gun off me." She growled.

"If you want to make it out of here alive, you better go along with me. Ready?" Amelia breathed deeply. If she didn't trust the woman she wouldn't have placed herself in such danger. Nevertheless, this position was her only opportunity at survival.

"Ready.

§

"Let me past you bastards or this one's dead!" Elnora screamed. A loud chatter broke out among the riot policemen, flabbergasted at a mother holding a gun to her daughter's head.

"Which way?" Amelia whistled through the corner of her mouth, exaggerating the shock horror mask for her face. "The smartest way would be left, where the police are. I'm not taking any chances of being shot by Rokas's men," Elnora replied almost casually.

"So, his name is Rokas!"

"Shut up! We'll talk later, if we're still alive that is." Here she was, her sweet innocent childhood mother, waving a gun and telling her to 'shut up'. Amelia was struggling to control her bewilderment; her life, really, was one big lie. Slowly but surely Elnora moved, making the odd threat here and there such as, 'Move and I'll shoot the bitch's brains out!" Or, 'It's loaded!"

Although moving aside willingly, the mix of forces knew the plan. Except they'd never be able to prove it. Amelia could see the headlines now, 'Psycho mother threatens life of fugitive daughter'. Only once they were a safe distance away did Elnora release Amelia from her grip.

"Well played. I guess I raised you well." Awkwardness filled the divide between them.

"What now?" Amelia asked, eager to move on.

"Let's just keep walk ..."

An ear piercing whistle pierced the night air. Elnora's knees buckled. She landed on the ground in a praying position, her face contorted by terror and dismay.

"Mum?"

The words were out before she could stop them, then she too was on her knees, laying Elnora back onto the cobblestones. Amelia felt around Elnora's back, feeling for the cause of her pain. Her hand slipped and shot straight out from under Elnora's sweat-shirt, her fingers coated in a thick maroon liquid. It had happened before, but now she was re-living it.

"Don't die on me." Amelia begged, her eyes tearful.

"The bullet hole's too big," Elnora replied softly, as though apologizing.

"I'll get help!"

"What good will that do? I'll be dead by time they arrive and you'll be arrested."

"Let me help you, Mum!"

"Listen to me Amelia, I've decided ... this is my time."

"What do you mean?"

"Cancer, Amelia. I have cancer." She continued. "We're talking a matter of long, painful months. This is good baby, my God it hurts but it's quick." Elnora struggled for breath, grasping Amelia's hand like she'd never let go.

"I know you want the truth, but right now wouldn't be good."

"I have to know, who are my real parents?"

"And you will. The truth will find you when you're ready. I'm sorry, I was never a good mum, but I always loved you. G ... go to my sister, Corinne Butler. She'll put you back on your path to freedom."

A final breath and Elnora's eyes closed, the look of terror replaced by peace and tranquillity. The street was quiet, the attackers had fled. It wasn't raining any more. In her hand she held a letter that Elnora had given her, with a sticky note dangling from the corner. She would open it when free. Scrawled neatly in black ink on the sticky note she read, 'Where to find Corinne Butler'. Along with a set of instructions.

§

"I know you're out there, show yourself!"
Katherine Marino crouched behind a large boulder near the edge of a river, grateful to be alive, but not happy at being hunted like some animal. Daring to move she inched forward. The crunch of damp leaves and corroded twigs underfoot revealing her location.
"Do you think you can fool me, Katherine?" He screamed.
"You don't know me, why are you doing this?" She called out from behind the boulder.
"Special order from Mr White."
"Bastard…" She muttered under her breath.
"You're going to die Katherine," he said crudely.
"No, I'm not!"
His voice grew closer, becoming clearer as the seconds ticked by. There was a child-like giggle, and then not a word until...
"I can see you Katherine, but you can't see me."

§

24 hours earlier.

"I didn't kill the Gizzard girl. I don't know who did."
Rokas had plainly said. They were lounging in sun
chairs beside the pool. Without a word Rokas suddenly
took his leave, as though late for work. Katherine
dragged herself from the comfort of her chair and went
to the kitchen, looking for her butler Michael. She was
doubtless in severe need of another drink. Frustrated
with Michael's whereabouts she energetically invented a
sickening cocktail for herself then returned to her chair
for another hour of relaxation.

"Surely he killed her … that must mean someone else is
involved? Someone big in the business … but who?"
She murmured away to herself, not noticing that at the
rear end of the pool Michael was floating face down in
the water, now gradually changing colour. Michael's
corpse drifted up against the tiled walls. Katherine, in a
hysteric frenzy, hung over the edge, using all her might
to heave the body from the pool. She turned it face up.
The cause of death was a thin slice running from one
end of his Arabian neck to the other. In the back of her
mind she knew that no one wanted to kill Michael; sadly
Michael had become a diversion for the attacker. She
feared she was next …

§

The heavens were pouring again. Amelia grimaced at
every step. Like earlier, the thunder was calling, but
more ferociously. All she could think of was the suited
man who'd murdered her adopted parents: dead, gone,
both. Then her mind turned to Emma; dead and gone.
The short note was scrunched in her back pocket. She
unfolded it carefully then stopped walking, desperately
looking for shelter. After taking refuge under a nearby
bus stop, she made sure no one was in sight. Satisfied

the coast was clear she placed the note on her lap and read:

Corinne Butler, Knockholt

Amelia barely remembered her Aunt. She'd often wondered why Corinne had never visited the Gizzard home, now she knew why. It was clear that Corinne knew of the family burden. If only she could reach Knockholt; find some answers and finally set herself free of her family past. A wishful dream. To even set foot near the Kent area she'd require a car and some money. Public transport wasn't an option; she was a wanted criminal. Her thoughts were suddenly interrupted by a faint echo; a police siren, but was it coming for her?

The sirens were coming closer. She'd exhausted any energy she may have had left hours ago, she was famished and thirsty, couldn't run if she'd wanted to. About a quarter of a mile further on was a stretch of woods that would open out onto the main roads, but what would she do from there? Where would she go? Where would she sleep? Who could she turn to for protection? Elnora and Cody had died shielding someone who wasn't a blood relation. Emma had been shot dead … now it was her turn to face the killer.

§

It would shortly be dark. Moonlight would soon light up her shelter. Katherine cried, she didn't want to die. She didn't want it to end like this. In the past twenty-four hours she'd been hunted down by an attacker who prided himself on representing Rokas White. She couldn't pinpoint his location; the forest was wild, life was dangerous when surrounded by the night. At one time they'd been head to head rivals in the business. Then she'd slipped up and played the fool ... she'd trusted Rokas White, let him in. Somewhere beyond the trees were the main roads, which she planned to reach before sunrise. This would mean more human faces, the chance of safety and security in numbers; surely this man wouldn't gun her down in broad daylight ... in front of witnesses? Would he?

§

Daughter's Downfall.

Newspaper report.
Yesterday evening revealed yet another body to be added to the Gizzard family grave. Cameras rolled as Amelia Gizzard was held at gunpoint by her own mother, Elnora Jane Gizzard. The pair fled east. Minutes later the body of Elnora Gizzard was found by the forces on the scene. Autopsy revealed bullet wounding, assumed inflicted by Amelia Gizzard. Suspicions were first raised three months earlier when police found June Gizzard fighting for her life on the floor of her aunt's flat. A month on an anonymous call led police to the house of Cody Gizzard, found deceased in the front room of his small home in West Sussex.
Amelia is wanted on three accounts of murder and one of attempted murder. Charles Fisher has made an appeal to the public. 'If you happen to see Amelia Gizzard, wherever you are, whatever you are doing, do not approach. She is considered armed and very dangerous. We strongly urge, if you do spot her call 999 right away and wait for the police to arrive.'
Are we dealing with the work of a monster?

§

The sun rose into the early day, masked by a dense fog engulfing the empty streets. The bus driver tapped his fingers against the dashboard in a quick, agitated motion. He lifted the glass barrier that separated him from the passengers and peered towards the back of the bus, empty; as he'd expected. The only life around today seemed to be him, and that freak that had passed out in the bus-stop.

"Are you getting on the bus or what?" He snarled for the fifth time.

"W-what?" She mumbled in and out of consciousness.

"I said … are you getting on the bus?" Amelia grunted and rolled over, light shivers radiating her body.

"Weirdo!" He barked. Once the doors of the bus were closed, it skidded away hurriedly. Spraying Amelia with what remained of yesterday's rain.

Amelia woke up with blurred vision, her back stiff from a night in the bus stop, the sun had now excelled itself above the clouds, glimmering with beauty and bringing light to the city of London. The fog had dispersed. It was a fine day; but not for her. She made some mental notes and instructions on getting through the day's events alive, hike through the wild forest hoping that it may lead her out onto the main roads, but then she'd need to find food and water. With the note containing her aunt's details still folded in the palm of her hand she used all her upper body strength to carry her worn legs to the ground.

Amelia began her never-ending walk, not knowing exactly where she was going or how she would get there. But one thing was for sure; she wasn't going to sit and wait for death.

§

Katherine slowly opened her eyes and rubbed damp leaves between her finger and thumb. The scent of pine hit her senses and she sprang to her feet, suddenly remembering were she was, and why she was here. She felt infuriated with herself that she'd allowed sleeping time whilst the killer still lingered about somewhere among the trees. Searching for her. Waiting for her.

She suddenly realised how early the sun had set and how exposed she was to her killer. She knew that in order to stay alive she must keep moving and find a trail to lead her out of the woodlands and onto the main roads, where safety waited for her. But how to do that with a murderer on her tail? Katherine understood why she'd never forgotten what had been over-heard on that first meeting when she'd supposedly 'left'; it still sent shivers down her spine. She must have been sensed eavesdropping on the conversation, after all it was the whole cause of this situation. Rokas would never be the type to simply kill someone he didn't like, there had to be a motive. He would be wise enough to know, that after what had been written in the papers and said by the press, he couldn't risk any more random killings.
"I know you're still there Katherine." The man's voice boomed from nowhere. It had been this way all night, his calls floating about with the noise of birds and animals.

He was close, she could feel it. She also felt imprisoned, seeing no route that wouldn't expose her. Deciding on her only possible route to survival, she began crawling towards the river that flowed east, but would it take her to the main roads?
"I'm getting warmer, aren't I?"

She slithered into the icy water, trembling; no time for her body to adjust to the water temperature as it would only delay her chance of getting away safely. If pneumonia wasn't to finish her off, then the man would, giving Rokas White his victory. She could picture the smug smile on his face. She wouldn't let it happen. Without a second thought or glance, she plunged her head below the water's surface and let the current wash her away from the murderer; away from danger…

§

Amelia had ambled through the woods for what seemed like several hours; it was mid-day and the sun was searing more than ever. On a day like this she would normally sit at the beach sipping on cold lemonade. She was beginning to miss the comfort of her barred pub, where she'd been sheltered and out of the way. If she hadn't left that day Elnora may still be breathing. It was Amelia they were searching for; Elnora had simply confused the trigger.

"Forgive me." Amelia mouthed to the clouds, her tongue dry from de-hydration. The sound of running water! Amelia stepped off the trail and headed towards the river. She knew it was the wrong thing to do but she was critically suffering from dehydration and if she didn't act soon …

§

Katherine silently cried in anguish as her leg struck solid rock. She was struggling to keep her head above water, unable to concentrate. She gasped for breath, still being swept along by the surge of the water. She felt paralyzed with exhaustion; cuts and bruises had appeared all over her skin. She didn't even know how long she had been afloat. Her eyes widened and her jaw dropped.

Katherine yelled desperately; she knew it was the end of the road for her. A small distance away was a pile of rubble and debris at least fifteen feet high, the water exiting through small gaps at the bottom of the heap. Unfortunately not wide enough for a human to slip through. Now there was no escape. Nobody knew her location or her plight. Katherine was imagining people's faces as they struggled to lift her decomposing corpse out of the river.

'Rokas White, you bastard,' was all she could think as she headed straight for her end.

§

Amelia bent down and slurped the fresh water greedily, overlooking the fact that it could be harmful. She suddenly stopped and spat in disgust, the water was far from fresh. It had a distinctive taste she'd come across as a little girl, when she'd fallen from a tree and bitten her tongue … fresh blood; but why would blood be mixed in with the water from the river?

"Oh my God!" Amelia screamed as she toppled forwards into the river. She knew why.

At the foot of the river, wedged between two rocks was a person. Floating on her back with her head barely above the water. Soaking red hair clung tightly to her head, but it was easy to notice that her eyes were closed. Was she dead or had she lost consciousness? Amelia struggled to clutch onto some support but was forced along towards the mountain of rocks, bricks, and rubble. "I … I'm c … coming." She struggled to shout, as she was dragged up and down. Slightly blinded, Amelia reached out for the floating body. Despite the freezing conditions the woman's skin felt warm. Her touch provided a wake up call; the woman's eyes opening as screamed in panic.

"It's okay; I'm going to get you out of here!" Amelia exclaimed. The woman nodded. Amelia understood that no matter who this woman was she was in the same danger that Amelia had been in … past and present. She didn't want to die.

§

"Another one relating to the Gizzard case, I'm guessing?" Amanda sighed.

"You guessed correctly." Charles replied.

"Mother?"

"Right again."

"I spoke to her over the phone when Amelia did a runner. She seemed ignorant and acted like we were not taking the situation seriously."

"Are you sleeping?" Charles asked quickly.

"Why?"

"Because I'm worried about you."

"Do you always bring your personal worries to work with you?" She snapped at him.

"If it involves one of my friends then I suppose so." He said calmly.

"We're not friends, Charles," she corrected.

"Oh, come on, I hate it when you call me Charles!"

"What are you trying to do here?"

"Trying to be nice. You're always so closed up! You don't let anyone in."

"That's my choice."

"It's the wrong choice."

"That's rich, coming from you." She laughed.

"Look, I've made plenty of wrong choices in life and I've accepted them so why can't you?"

"Don't start again, okay?"

"But, you know the worst mistake I ever made ?"

"What?"

"I let you get away." A twinkle in his left eye. He was falling for her, again. How had she been so idiotic as to not notice the way he looked at her, the way he spoke around her, the way he cared.

"Wh … where was she found?" Amanda asked, clearing her throat, disregarding him completely.

"Why are you changing the subject?"

"I just asked you a question, where was she found?"

Charles shook his head looking slightly hurt, and then continued. "You know that run down pub, the Kings Arms?"

"Yes."

"Well, we believe Amelia Gizzard was hiding there. She was spotted at a library about five minutes away where she'd ran and bumped into her mother. When surrounded by police her mother pointed a gun at her and threatened to shoot unless the police let them past. About ten minutes later Elnora was shot; her body was found just around the corner from the pub. My guess is she was trying to take Amelia back there and Amelia shot her. She was shot near the heart and would have died within seconds."

"Anything else?"

"She was dying of cancer."

"Poor thing …"

"I know, right?"

"Charles?"

"Yes?"

"Why would she shoot her own mother?"

"That's the question everybody asks, why her father? Why her mother? Why did she try and stab her niece? I asked around. Apparently when the twins where little the family wasn't what you would call normal; Mum and Dad always fighting and so on. Personally, I believe Emma Gizzards death sparked something in Amelia, destroyed some sort of sisterhood confidence and support they'd shared when younger. They must have been close. Twins usually are."

"What If I told you that Amelia didn't do any of those things?"

"Not this again, do you have evidence?"

"No, just a very strong gut feeling."

"Well this case can't run on gut feelings, the sooner the girl is found the quicker she can be put behind bars and the case can be closed – God, I feel like I've got a permanent migraine!"

"Fine, have it your way, but mark my words … I'll prove you wrong."

§

They had scrambled out onto flat land; any longer and the woman would certainly have died. She was a canvas of cuts and bruises. The woman fidgeted away from Amelia's grasp, body trembling.

"Please, calm down!" Amelia said, offering an arm to support the woman who was limping with every step.

"I …- need t … to g..get away!" The woman cried, attempting to run.

"You didn't get into that river accidentally, did you?" Amelia queried, cautiously. The woman stopped running and shook her head.

"H … he's still out there. I need to get out of this forest."

"He?"

"The man's who's trying to kill me!" She screamed at Amelia. Thousands of birds erupted from the trees, then a rustling sound.

"Get down!" Amelia hissed, herding the woman towards a line of bushy plants. The woman obeyed. A male voice, a recognisable voice.

"Bastard …" she whispered.

"You know him?" The woman mouthed.

"Indeed."

"How?"

"Because … he killed my father."

"What's your father's name?"

"Well, he wasn't my real father, but his name was Cody Gizzard."

"That means … you're Amelia!"

"Keep your voice down!"

"Sorry, I just know a lot about you."

The voice visited them again, this time more angered. Amelia stared in confusion.

"I've had enough you silly little cow, show yourself!"

"What's your name?" She asked warily.

"Katherine." She muttered. "Katherine Marino."

"I've read about you Katherine. You don't seem to see eye to eye with Rokas White."

"How do you know?"

"You have a lot of spare time when you're a fugitive."

"We have to get out of here Amelia, this man will kill us."

"You think I don't know that?"

"On the count of three we run?"

"That seems the only option."

"Ready?"

Amelia nodded, squeezing Katherine's hand.

"One, two …."

Katherine screamed in terror as she felt herself being pulled out of the bush, a pair of strong hands twisted in her hair.

"Get off her!" Amelia yelled, suddenly grabbing Katherine's ankles and using all her strength to tear her away from the attacker.

"Stay out of this Amelia," the man commanded furiously.

"I said get off her!"

Amelia released Katherine, now struggling desperately in the man's arms. She couldn't relive another murder, she just couldn't. Without warning the man found himself plummeting to the grass, Amelia's fingernails scratching away at his beady eyes.

"Let me deal with her, you don't understand who she is."

"Don't listen to him Amelia!"

Amelia jumped to her feet exhausted and dragged a weeping Katherine from the ground. The man just inches away ready to pounce.

"Run!"

§

"Don't stop, I can see the roads!"

"He's right behind us Amelia!"

She wasn't lying; he was right on their tail, sprinting at top speed. Amelia felt a rush of relief as they exited the woods, then an attack of horror; he wasn't giving up just yet.

"Watch out!" She shrieked, forcefully throwing herself and Katherine out of the path of a speeding car. The car slipped from the road and headed for their attacker. The driver had clearly lost control, and in no time at all collided with Rokas's man. He spun through the air in a triple flip, and then fell to the ground, his cranium shattered. Blood sprayed a trail to where his body landed, skidding roughly. He lay motionless at Amelia's feet before murmuring three short words.

"Don't trust her." His eyes fluttered then closed..

§

A hysterical elderly woman climbed from the car. Slowly she walked over to the corpse, lying twisted and turned.

"What have I done?" She sobbed.

"Good riddance." Katherine spat.

"How can you say that, he's dead!"

"Did you realise he was chasing us?" Amelia interrupted.

"Of course not!" Amelia and Katherine exchanged understanding looks.

"We need the car," they both said awkwardly.

"What?"

"We need to get away from here."

"You know what, take it. It's making me sick just looking at it. I'll tell the police I was hiking and found the man like this, yes … they will believe that won't they?" The woman asked nervously, tears in her eyes.

"I would think so …" Amelia lied.

"Here are the keys, hurry up!" She flung a set of keys to Amelia. They hopped into the car, Amelia driving, Katherine in the passenger seat.

"I'll drop you off at a hospital, I can't come in."

"Good, once I'm done with him he's going to wish he was never born."

"That's how I feel but I need to know something. Why was that man after you?"

The sight of Katherine's face was one she had seen before, fright and worry but also … pure loathing.

"Because … I made a deal with the devil."

§

"This is bullshit, Charles!" Amanda chuckled, shoving the newspaper away.

"So, you're saying she didn't kill Elnora, Cody, and Emma?"

"Exactly!"

"What other logical explanation is there?"

"I would tell you, but you'd only doubt me."

111

"No, come on." Charles sat back. "I feel like laughing today."

"I've been researching," she said, ignoring his previous comment. "When Elnora pointed the gun at Amelia …"

"Self Defence?"

"Let me finish!"

"Okay, okay!"

"So, as I was saying … when Elnora pointed the gun at Amelia, I did some asking around; turns out that three ex- cons were spotted at the crime scene … Paul Lace, Jeremy Rayne, and Leighton Nile."

"So what? You can't go around accusing someone of being involved in a crime simply because they've done time before."

"Well, if you don't class working for Rokas White as a bad thing, then you're off your head, nuts"

"Get to the point." Charles sighed.

"So, I called in Leighton Nile."

"Why him?"

"He looked the most fragile of the men." She admitted.

"And?"

"I asked him why he'd been there. He told me he was simply out with two friends and they came across the park to see what was happening. I noticed he was twitching and sweating, so I accused him of hiding something and threatened to put his ass behind bars before he could say Rokas White."

"So what did he say?"

"He said that Mr White was interested in the Gizzard family, and that he and Cody used to be good pals."

"Used to be?"

"That's just it, isn't it? So I start digging into the family past. I discovered that Elnora was checked into Great Ormond Street hospital with a stab wound near the uterus.

Rokas White and Cody Gizzard had taken her there which confirms Rokas White was there."

"And you think that's why they became distant."

"Sort of. I continued researching. During the interview Cody said that Elnora had been attacked on the streets; but there was no evidence to support that either Cody or Rokas had done it. But anyway, two years later Elnora suddenly gives birth to twins; I wanted to see where they were born so I could figure out if Rokas White had been there at the time. Now, obviously, this seems slightly far-fetched, but I contacted several hospitals around London and all deny knowing an Elnora Gizzard. So I go further, getting hold of family photos."

"What are you trying to say?"

"That the girls bear no resemblance to either Cody or Elnora. There are no birth certificates or reords they were ever born. I then got in touch with every orphanage I could find in London; all deny ever having had an Amelia or Emma. I dug through old newspaper clippings on the internet. One article in particular focused on a Cecilia Jane."

"And ..?"

"It said that her new-born twin girls had gone missing, and that she was accusing Rokas White of kidnap. I've been trying to piece it together. I believe Rokas stabbed Elnora, whereafter she couldn't have children. I think that to make it up to the couple Rokas took Cecilia Jane's children and gave or even sold them, to Cody and Elnora Gizzard, basically an illegal adoption. I'm certain that Amelia and Emma are not in any way related to either Cody or Elnora."

"You're just assuming they're not their children."

"It's a possibility. I mean, the twin girls were never found!"

"Well, I'll give it to you for all the research, but isn't that even more reason for Amelia to have lost it, killed her sister and then Cody and Elnora?"

"Yes, but I doubt it. Really, Charles what I do want to is to speak to this Rokas White, try and find out about this 'dodgy deal' of so long ago."

"I'm afraid you can't do that. You're biting off more than you can chew with little evidence."

"Fine, but like I said, I will prove you wrong." Shaking her head she delved into her rucksack and produced a square piece of laminated text.

"Take a look at this. When you're ready to think outside the box get back to me."

§

The first hour of the ride Amelia and Katherine spent in silence, both appreciating they still had their lives. The old Hummer drove on; trees and scenery zoomed by. Amelia could only wonder when she'd be able to shut her eyes and wake up in a world that wasn't out to kill her. Something wasn't right. From the moment she'd set her hands on the steering wheel the three words had found a 'niche' in her gut. 'Don't trust her.'

She turned to Katherine, snoring peacefully. What was this woman hiding? Why was she being hunted?

"Katherine." She snored on.

"Katherine, wake up!"

"What? What?" Katherine mumbled, slowly opening her eyes.

"What did you mean by, 'I made a deal with the devil'?"

"Do you really want to know?"

"Yes."

"Okay … well, this is awkward."

"Why?"

"Because, I … I made a deal with Rokas White to take your late father's fortune."

"Wait … what?"

"I'm telling the truth."

"But I'd have to be dead for you to do that, because, if I'm not mistaken, I'd inherit it all."

"Exactly. They're after you Amelia."

"You think I don't know that?"

"I'm sorry."

"No, don't you dare. I get it all now. I get why he killed Cody and Elnora, even Emma. He wanted us all dead. I'm next aren't I?"

Katherine nodded sympathetically.

"That means you; you didn't stop him killing them."

"No, I didn't. He won't stop at it Amelia, I mean it. I even told him I'd personally see to it you're killed. But he told me not to, which means he wants to do it himself."

"I saved your life …"

"I know, and I couldn't be more grateful." she whispered shamefully. Amelia slammed her foot onto the brakes, sending Katherine face first into the dashboard.

"What in hell are you doing?" Katherine hissed, rubbing a growing lump on her forehead.

"Get. Out." Amelia took a deep breath, fighting back the tears.

"Oh, come on, we're in the middle of nowhere!"

"I said, get out!"

"No, you can't do this to me."

"Right then." Unbuckling her seat belt she swung open the driver's door and climbed out. With balled fists and heavy feet she stomped around the car and around to the passenger door.

"Amelia, calm down!" Katherine begged. Amelia gripped a strong hold of fine hair and slowly dragged her from the relative safety of the car onto the emptiness of the side-walk.

"Please, Amelia, don't leave me here." Katherine sobbed. With tearful eyes Amelia raised a hand, preparing to slap. A rare sane moment restrained her. *You're still human Amelia, be the better person …* the voice in her head rung.

"You know what, Katherine?"

"What?"

"I could have left you to drown in that river …"

Amelia vanished into the misty night, engine revving, leaving a startled Katherine rocking back and forth in the bitter weather. Somewhere out there was a callous man with a heart as cold as ice. Once the news of an employee's sudden death reached Rokas White there'd be no turning back. Katherine had missed a grim death by inches, but deep down she knew it wouldn't be long. He'd find her and amplify her death sentence with torture. She'd never be able to marry and have children, never die peacefully in the comfort of her own home. No … in the dead of night with no one to hold, she'd die a slow, painful death.

Amelia continued on her journey, too exhausted to think of Katherine or how she'd find Knockholt. What she needed was time to rest and recover. But she knew that once she closed her eyes she'd be as vulnerable as a gazelle unaware of its predator about to pounce … Rokas White. Her eyelids began sagging. Seconds later they hung heavily … ready to close but never wanting to open again.

§

She knelt on her knees, a ringing screech piercing her delicate ears. No more than five years old, when the world was at its best … but she at her worst. She was in an opaque room with four corners pointing outwards, in each corner a silent flaring medieval torch.

"You know, you wouldn't be here if you'd only listened to me …" Emma's voice emerged from thin air. As the voice grew louder a human figure swiftly formed. It stepped out from the shadow of the first corner. Emma took hold of the torch and gave a frightening cry. The torch flickered, then died, plummeting Emma's corner into darkness.

"Were you worth dying for?" Elnora asked, suddenly appearing from the second corner.
"Eln … Mum, please!"
Elnora dropped the torch; the second corner fell into darkness.
"She's right Amelia. We all died because of you." Cody laughed spitefully and launched his torch in Amelia's direction; it stopped midway and vanished. Cody's corner evaporated into the black. June suddenly appeared from the final corner, but instead of remaining still she stepped forward until she was face to face with Amelia. Her jaw lowered and she let out an eerie sound … the sound of a beeping horn and skidding tires. Amelia's eyes shot open as her body was shoved forward, twisted in pain. It was as though she'd somehow left her body and floated into the air. She was looking at the ground below at a scene of two cars. One mangled and ablaze, the other untouched. In the light of the fiery inferno she watched an injured woman being pulled from the mangled car and lugged across to the car that had caused the incident. It was her. But who was pulling her? Who had not driven away? This person could be saving her life, but … at the same time, be ending her life.

§

"Are you waking up?"
Amelia groaned as her body sprang to life with alarm.
"Now now, you'll only hurt yourself."
"What is this place?"
"You don't remember me?" The small woman asked in surprise. At that moment a tiny sparrow fluttered its wings, landing on the inside windowsill.
"Little fella's got a broken wing; they always seem to show up here." She gently cupped the sparrow in the palm of her hands.
"Who are you?"
The aroma of roasting pork reminded Amelia she needed food and water, soon. The woman noticed immediately.
"You poor thing. I bet you haven't eaten properly since you ran away?" She tutted sympathetically.
"Please … tell me who you are?" Amelia pleaded.
"One more guess?"
Those three words triggered her memory. A spring breeze wafted into the room, easing her burns and bruises. A pleasant feeling came over her, warming her heart and soul. In the left hand corner of the room stood an elegant double brass bed, the walls were covered with roses, spread and spotted over cream paint, the type of room Emma would love and praise. It was the cottage considered a house, the place where she and her sisters had spent generous summers. There was a back garden with fresh growing grass and a tyre swing that … at least she hoped … was still there.
"Forgive me, Auntie Corinne!" Amelia giggled. "It happens from time to time."

Corinne was small with chubby red cheeks, her short golden hair aged into grey curls. She wore a spotted cooking apron over her knitted cardigan. As the only sister to Elnora the pair were entirely different.

"How did I get here?"

"Well, you had your driving lights on full beam and so did I. I turned mine off, you didn't, and … boom. We crashed. I pulled you from the car, oh, I recognised you immediately! We drove off and, well, we're here!"

"You knew I was already on my way to see you?"

"I thought you may be, considering the direction you were heading."

Amelia nodded.

"Now …" Corinne said uneasily, settling herself on the edge of the bed, "I believe you need some answers."

Again she nodded.

"First, I need you to know something."

"What is it?"

"I don't believe a word the media and papers are saying about you, I know you're innocent."

"Thank you." Amelia said, choking up.

"You don't need to thank me."

"Corinne?"

"Yes?"

"Did you hear about Elnora?"

"Yes."

"How are you dealing with it?"

"When it's our time it's our time. She was dying Amelia but I suspect you already knew that. Am I correct?"

"Yes, she told me before she died."

"Right, now let's get you fed and washed and then we'll have a cuppa and a good chat."

"Corinne, pardon me for being rude but I would appreciate it if we could kind of talk now? I've waited a long time for answers I never thought I'd get."

Corinne shuffled uncomfortably, as though about to say something that should never be said.

"Okay." She took a deep breath. "What do you want to know?"

Amelia struggled. What to say next? After such a long time hiding from the world she'd need to ease out of her shell in order to drive her life back into normality.

"You've been away from civilization for a long time, haven't you?" Corinne asked.

"I'm trying ..."

"I know, but this is just a normal conversation, relax."

"No, Corinne, this isn't a normal conversation and we both know it."

"Maybe, but think of it as revisiting memories? Everyone talks about memories don't they?"

Amelia closed her eyes, imagining herself in college, chatting happily alongside Emma.

"You start." Amelia smiled.

"Where you're from?" Corinne frowned.

"Yes, where I'm from."

"Well, dear, I'm afraid I'm not much use to you there, but I can tell you how you ended up in the Gizzard's care?"

"Yes, let's start with that, eh?"

"By now I bet you're familiar with the name, Rokas White?" Her speech was strained, as though the words 'Rokas White' hurt her inside.

"Do I know Rokas White? He killed Elnora, he killed Emma and he killed Cody, and now ... he's after me."

"Believe it or not, Cody and Rokas used to be inseparable."

"You're joking?"

"On my sister's grave."

"Then why would he set out to kill him."

"Because your fath ..."

"He was not my father!"

"But he still existed," Corinne murmured.

"I'm sorry, please carry on." She snuffled, again with the tensed shoulders; this was tough, really tough.

"Well, as I was saying, Cody had something that belonged to Rokas, and still does to this day."

"It's money isn't it?"

"How did you guess?"

"Well, there was this woman running, got herself in a bit of bother. I sorted some things out for her and she told me that 'I'm rich'."

"She was right Amelia, I'm certain you've inherited a good lump of money."

"Of cursed money."

"Maybe. Who was the girl running from?"

"Rokas."

"Was she connected in any way to Rokas's money?"

"Rokas's money?"

"Well, I'd think so."

"But why did Cody have Rokas's money? Why do I have Rokas's money?"

"This is the tricky part."

"Why?"

"You remember, I was never much of a visitor to the house?"

"Because you were the only one who knew their secret?"

"Right, and I never approved of it one bit. I could never bring myself to trust him."

"Rokas?"

"Yes, Rokas."

"Why?"

"Because he stabbed my sister, Elnora."

"He what? Hang on a minute … if he and Cody were inseparable why would he stab Elnora?"

"Rokas and Cody said it was an accident, but me, I don't know."

"Bastard."

"Tell me about it. She always wanted children. As a little girl she'd have those dolls. Oh, she just couldn't wait. He practically took away her life."

"So where do me and Emma end up in all of this?"

"Now, to make it up to your Mum and your Dad, from out of nowhere Rokas appeared with a pair of gorgeous new-born girls; twins, of course."

"Those twins … me and Emma?"

"Right. So when this man appears offering the babies I tell Elnora 'He stabbed you, there has to be a catch. He must want money or something. She tells me 'No, he's repaying me, I guess'. But you must understand Amelia; babies aren't toys. Babies aren't something you just illegally deal around. I didn't know where you and Emma had come from; I never knew how he got hold of you. I tried to track your real mother and father. My plan was to steal you one night and take you back to where you rightfully belonged."

"Anything else?" Amelia asked, tears in her eyes. She cupped Corinne's wrinkled hands in hers.

"It turned out, in the end, my theory was correct. Rokas White did want money. And we're not talking thousands or even hundreds of thousands; we're talking four to five million."

"They could never have afforded that, especially at the time!"

"Exactly. But due to circumstances at the time i.e. the stabbing, Rokas was willing to let Cody pay off the money until you girls reached sixteen."

"And what happened?"

"Cody stopped the payments after the second year."

"But what then?"

"Rokas flipped. He stormed over and demanded Cody give the money, or give up you and Emma."

"So, he refused to give us up, that's why we still lived with him?"

"No, my darling, he *wanted* to give you up. It was Elnora who protected you and chased Rokas from the house. She threatened him with death. You and Emma were never let out of her sight. Eventually Rokas stopped visiting."

"So he's returned ..."

"To claim what is rightfully his. I knew he was never gone forever. I knew the day he came back all hell would break loose, and that's why I could never visit, because I couldn't look at both of your innocent faces and believe things would be okay. It was always going to be this way Amelia. This is not your fault!"

"But Cody and Elnora died to save me, they loved me."

"It is because of them that you're in this position. I'll tell you now, Elnora loved you like you were her own, but Cody was in a sort of debt with her. He wanted rid of you and Emma the moment you were dropped on their doorstep."

"I understand." Amelia nodded, although she didn't, couldn't, understand much anymore.

"What you need to do is gather evidence that'll prove your innocence."

"Like what?"

"You need something that'll prove you didn't murder Emma, Cody or Elnora."

"What about June?"

"You need a confession, but that won't be possible. Like I said, you need to collect this evidence and then, once the air is clear, hopefully June will spill the truth."

"Corinne. I know full well how I can get evidence."

"How?"

"It's a risk, but it seems the only way."

"What is it?"

"It's time I pay a visit to Mr White."

§

Amanda gulped greedily from her plastic cup, the coffee masking the smell of stale alcohol on her breath. The previous night had shown her what she'd been missing out on. London was a destination to party and mingle … she may have even made a friend or two. Unfortunately today would not be as promising. Leads had a habit of not showing themselves lately; the case was progressing slowly and becoming wearisome. How Amelia Gizzard was still alive she didn't know, but she hoped it stayed that way.

Amanda was expecting the office to be fairly quiet this morning; she needed the day to drift by in a blur to cure her splitting headache. Was it the alcohol? Or just life in general?

"Amanda." Charles called, jogging over to the other side of the narrow corridor.

"What is it? I'm kind of busy." She lied. She wanted to avoid contact with the man as much as possible, having noticed recently he was falling for her. It couldn't work. It wouldn't work because he'd betrayed her, and she would keep a grudge because love hurts, because love chooses its victims wisely.

"Well, you must've been busy last night." He said, fidgeting in his pocket then producing a tube of soft mints and ripping them open. "Here." He forced one into her hand and pointed at it. "You stink."

"I'm flattered."

"Not that It matters anyway. You might as well pack up and go home."

"Why?"

124

"Something's happened; I'm not obliged to say."

"Come with me, we can grab something to eat?"

"Really, I would but I have to stay for a while, there's a big investigation and I'm expected to answer some questions. I really would like to grab something to eat sometime." He whispered, looking slightly disappointed.

"Please tell me, I promise I won't tell a soul."

"Really?"

"Yes, really. Now, come on I've got a Big Mac calling my name." Normally Charles would have smiled, instead his facial expression grew morose.

"You know Rita Rose Don't you?"

"The Forensic girl, the one who examined Emma Gizzard's body."

"Yes, well something's happened."

"What is it? Spit it out."

"She's gone."

"That's it, just left?"

"Arrested."

"No way? Ron, are you serious?"

"Let's just say she's probably being charged as we speak."

§

"Do you have a death wish or something?" Corinne croaked anxiously.

"What else am I supposed to do; I can't just sit here and do nothing." Amelia replied.

"Yes, you can, you can stay with me."

"No, Corinne, you know I have to do this."

"But why?"

"I need him off my back. I need to know who my real parents are."

"You think you can walk in there and say 'leave me alone?' He'll probably shoot you on the spot."

"Maybe he will, maybe he won't."

"Anything I can do to change your mind?"

"Unless you can offer me freedom, then no."

"When will you do it?"

"Tomorrow. Tonight I'll establish where he lives."

"No need for that."

"Why not?"

"I know where he lives. He's been living there ever since you were born. I've been right under his nose all this time and he hasn't realised."

"Where?"

"Four doors down from here."

"Just four doors down?" She laughed nervously. "Yes, just four bloody doors down."

"How has not seen you?"

"More like how have I not seen him? Simple. He has his own little servants to do everything; if he's not in the 'white manor' then he's somewhere in his black limo. That's what takes him everywhere."

"How will I know if he's home?"

"The black limo will be parked up outside, obviously."

"Okay."

"But seriously, are you going to just walk up and knock on the front door?"

"Sounds the easiest way." Amelia shrugged.

"You're crazy."

"I know." Amelia said, taking hold of Corinne's hand once again.

"You don't have to worry about me Corinne, worry about yourself, just for once, okay?"

"Why should I worry about myself?"

"You say he hasn't realised you're living here. I think you're completely wrong."

"And why's that?"

"Because he will have been watching you for a long time; if you ask me, he's probably watching right now."

126

June sketched on the note-pad she'd flung open on her desk, oblivious to the teacher's presence.

"June, it's clear you don't want to be here, so why don't you just leave?" The teacher barked. Her classmates burst into a fit of giggling and gossip.

"You know what?" June smiled broadly as she closed her secret notepad and stood up from her desk. "I think I will." The laughter again.

"Get. Out!" The teacher screamed.

"Gladly." She snarled, and slammed the door.

"Carry on with your work!" the teacher ordered.

June strolled peacefully out the school main door. None of it mattered anymore … education, family. She knew that soon it would all be over. Her anticipation had gone on for too long. The detectives were stupid not to have realised that everything from her mouth was a complete lie. From the moment she'd framed her aunt Amelia it had been straight into foster care; no one wanted her 'damaged' ways in their household. She'd restrained her enthusiasm for far too long. Everyone had thought they could see through her; things were far from so, it was a complete reverse. It always was. No one would have expected it; no one would see it coming. It was finally her time, her time to show the world what she was made of.

§

The White Manor

"No Corinne, you know I have to do this."

"But why?"

"I need to get him off my back. I need to know who my real parents are."

"You think you can walk in there and say 'leave me alone?' he will probably shoot you on the spot."

"Maybe he will, but maybe he won't."

"Is there anything I can do to change your mind?"

"Unless you can offer me freedom, then no."

Rokas White removed his headset, smiling wickedly. No sooner done than he turned towards Katherine Marino, cowering in the corner, weeping for her life.

"What are you going to do to me?"

"Isn't it obvious, you need to die Katherine."

"Why?"

"Don't treat me like an idiot; you're going to die because you know," he said coldly.

"I'm begging you." With her hands in a pleading position Katherine suddenly crawled forward.

"Don't touch me!" Rokas spat angrily, shoving Katherine away with his left foot.

"You worthless piece of shit!" He screamed. "It would've been easy if you'd just listened and kept your nose out of my business, but no. That's what you're like isn't it, Katherine? Always snooping around where you shouldn't, always hearing what shouldn't be heard, well, that won't happen anymore, not now, not ever." Rokas snapped his fingers. A lean, bony man entered the room, his vacant eyes surveying Katherine, curled up in her corner.

"Katherine, meet Paul Lace. He'll be accompanying you today."

"Is it time boss?"

"Yes, take her." Rokas ordered.

Paul Lace walked slowly, each step of his heavy boots causing Katherine to crawl backwards further into her corner … until, moments later her back found a solid wall. Seizing her by the hair Paul lifted her from the floor, and with one fluid movement roughly positioned her hands behind her back until finally she was restrained and unable to flee.

"Rokas, you can't do this!" Katherine cried as she was forcefully dragged from the room. Rokas was mute. "ROKAS!"

"Paul?" Rokas shouted. Paul grunted. "Make it slow …"

§

Most visualized The White Manor as a grand mansion with fountains endlessly gushing spring water, or smooth curved pathways leading to mature wooden doors with two brass handles hanging with pride. It was the complete opposite.

"What is this?" Amelia doubled over, choking with laughter. The house was a standard two storey building, built of corroding red bricks. In place of a curved pathway was a line of crumbling black tarmac separating two small patches of pale yellow grass. A dozen pairs of unattractive lime curtains were drawn at each window, blocking the inside view of the house. The inner portions of the grounds were sectioned off from a knee high brick wall which could easily be stepped over. At the corner of the wall, planted low into the ground, was an ancient piece of wood displaying three fading words … 'The White Manor'.

"All this time Corinne, I've been being hunted like a rat, a rat. By this man? This man who lives here!" Amelia spat through gritted teeth.

"The limo's there, which means he's there."

"How does he afford it?"

"Who knows?" Corinne paused and checked Amelia, whose confidence had lifted. "Are you ready?"

"Yes, I'm ready."

Amelia began ambling across the black tarmac. Corinne shouted. "Amelia!"

"What is it?"

"Don't make this the last time I see you, okay?"

"Okay."

"Goodbye, Amelia."

"Thank you for everything. I promise we'll see each other soon."

"Your mother would be so proud of you …"

She turned to reply but Corinne had gone; she was on her own once again. This time in enemy territory.

"This is it, Amelia." She muttered to herself, making her way up to the front door. She'd prepared to knock but held back at the blur of a man who'd appeared from behind the door, and then drawn closer until a whole body was visible and a pair of human eyes looked at her through the thin glass. Rokas White. Her heart skipped a beat.

"Open the door, face me," She yowled, barely knowing what she was doing.

"Gladly." Rokas mouthed. After a few seconds of unbolting the door swung open and smacked hard against the brick wall. The air from the house was as cold as ice. From what she could see the place was still and calm.

"Are you coming in?" What prevented her from running back was a year of long awaited vengeance drugging her mind. What stopped her was that finally she was face to face with the man who'd slaughtered her sister, Elnora and Cody. Amelia couldn't imagine how many more innocent people he'd had killed. This was it, this was her time.

§

"I've been expecting you." Rokas said energetically as she followed him into the living room. "Wait no, come into the kitchen. I'll make some tea."

Kitchen, Knives. Tea ... poisoned?

"Maybe I want to sit into the living room." Amelia spoke anxiously, stepping back from the kitchen.

"Have it your way." The living room had a similar aura to the flat she owned back in London; flaky crimson wallpaper lazily pasted up onto the crooked walls, the lifting carpet a dull, ash-grey colour. The only furniture an unappealing settee finished off with an old-fashion coal fire that looked as if it hadn't been lit since June had been born.

"Nice place."

"Thank you," Rokas replied.

"I was joking."

Rokas gave a hearty grin.

"Why are you smiling?"

"Take a seat." He gestured at the couch, ignoring her question.

"Who else is here? Hey, I bet you have one of your men upstairs ready to do me in, don't you?"

"Will you please sit down?" Rokas puffed, running a hand through his thick gold hair.

"I don't want to sit down."

"Stand then."

"You know what I'm going to ask, don't you?"

"Yes," he said quietly.

"Who the hell are you, and why are you trying to kill me?"

§

"Let's get one thing straight Amelia, my name is Rokas White, and I am not trying to kill you." He spoke softly.

"I know who you are, but that's bullshit. Bullshit. Bullshit." Amelia shook her head in anger, adrenaline pumping.

"It's not bullshit; I have no reason to kill you."

"The money." She stated.

"Your money."

"Yes, the money you want to get your filthy paws on."

"My money," he corrected, "but, aaaahh, I do not want it. It is rightfully yours."

"Why, trying to make up for taking me from my birth mother?"

"Now Ame …."

"Let me tell you something, okay?" Amelia cried furiously. "Elnora and Cody are dead, died trying to protect me from you … you killed them."

"You don't understand Amelia …"

"And Emma, I bet you killed her too."

"Amelia please hear me out …"

"You think money can make me forget what you did to me? You think I like this life? For months I've been forced to run and hide because I was set up by my own niece. And then I have someone like you on my tail. Live a life in my shoes and you'd see how I've been forced to live!"

"I did kill Elnora and I did kill Cody."

"Is that a confession?"

Rokas pitched forward and stared her up and down, his voice getting higher and much less amiable

"I killed Elnora, and I killed Cody … to protect you!"

"Wh … what?" Amelia croaked.

"They were bad people; they had to be dealt with, to stop them making your life a misery."

"Y …you, y … you bastard!"

Amelia threw herself forward, pointing her fist at Rokas, who avoided the attack then firmly gripped both her wrists in one hand.

"Listen to me!"

"I don't need to listen to you, you ruined my life!" Amelia spat in his face.

"I said listen to me; for crying out loud … listen to your father!"

§

The struggle ended; silence filled the air. Rokas slowly released his grip on her wrists and gradually lowered her to the floor.

"Will you sit down now?"

Amelia nodded, taking a seat next to him.

"You're my father?" She asked, trying to steady her breathing, to stem the tears.

"Yes, Amelia, I'm your father."

"If you're my father, it means Emma was your daughter, which means you killed your daughter." Amelia turned away, tears blinding her eyes.

"I didn't kill Emma. I killed Cody and Elnora to protect you. That money is rightfully mine, but I want you to have it."

"I don't want the money!"

"Then what do you want?"

"I want my life back."

"I can't give you back your old life Amelia, but I can give you a new one. You have enough money to change your name; we can move away together and make a new start."

"That's not good enough Rokas, I want a clear name. I want people to know I'm innocent. I don't want people thinking I murdered my family."

"They weren't your family."

"Well, where where you? Where where you when I needed you most? You weren't there, no, you were never there!"

"I was always there, always watching!"

"Watching isn't being. I want to know everything; who I am and who Emma was."

"Are you up for a long story?"

"I've been up for it all my life."

"Okay."

"Ready when you are."

Rokas quivered and paced the room several times before sitting down again.

"Your real name ... is Lillian Jones. Emma's real name is ... Lauren Jones. Your real mother's name ... is Cecelia Jones."

"What did you to Cecelia, what did you do to us?"

"Well, times were tough and the money wasn't just rolling in. I'd only spent a short time with Cecelia before breaking up, I was devastated. But then about five months later she comes back with a bump, said she wanted to settle down."

"But, you weren't in love were you?"

"No, we weren't, most nights we never spoke. And then when you and Emma were born things went bad, I hit my lowest point in life; became addicted to several types of drugs."

"But why?"

"It was Cecelia ... she hated me. Well, I had a job but most of the time I was blowing money on drugs, then I was fired when everyone realised what I was like. That's when I became desperate. I got in touch with an old friend and ... I'm so sorry Amelia."

"Carry on; I need to know it all."

"This guy's wife is unable to have children, because of me, because I stabbed her. So, I offered him you and Emma in exchange for a certain amount of money each year. Around midnight I crept into your room without Cecelia knowing and snatched up you and Emma, said my final goodbyes and dropped you off. When I came back Cecelia was standing over your cots crying her eyes out. She turned to me and started screaming 'What have you done with them'. I said I was sorry and ran from her."

"What next?"

"Well, I went back, but Elnora threatened me. She'd become obsessed with you and Emma, then the Gizzards moved away and I never saw either of you again; until now." Rokas smiled gently, placing a hand softly on Amelia's shoulder.

"Get away from me!" She cringed.

"Forgive me."

"F ... forgive you? How could I ever forgive you?"

"Because, I can give you something you've wanted for a long time!"

"Oh, can you now? And what's that?" She sneered.

Of course there was no proof, but it felt like the puzzle had been pieced nevertheless. If he was her father then she'd been bred from a satanic monster. All this time Cecelia Jones had been deprived of her children; it was likely she'd even assumed them dead. Amelia couldn't expose her weak side to Rokas, she'd need to progress beyond him and get away as soon as possible. Rokas wiped his tears on the sleeve of his tailored suit. The atmosphere was prickly. Amelia shivered, it was freezing. Rokas lifted a hand from his side, the hand floated forwards and landed gently on her cheek. She didn't refuse the gesture; she knew it wouldn't be wise. And then he squeaked something, so quiet it made her ask again. "What's that?"

"I can give you your sister."

§

"I'd like to think you know why you're here," Amanda said. Rita Rose rocked her head back and forth. Her body quivering with fear… of what?

"We were good friends you and I, Rita? Weren't we?"

Again the creepy nodding.

"Then, can you take me through what you did that day, and what made you do it?"

"But I've already told you everything!"

"I know, I know. Just so I'm clear."

"Okay, well, as you know I was doing the autopsy."

"On who?"

"Do I really need to say?"

"Just to clarify."

"Emma Gizzard."

"In your report you said it was Emma Gizzard."

"Yes, I did."

"And was it Emma Gizzard; did you in fact, ever at all, see the body of Emma Gizzard?"

"It was not Emma Gizzard on the table. I've never seen Emma Gizzard in my life."

§

"How dare you!"

"I'm telling you the truth; I can give you your sister. Emma is alive!" Rokas protested.

"Emma is dead!" She erupted, hurling a glass ornament at him. He threw himself to the floor barely avoiding the shattered glass.

"I can show you," he panted.

"How?"

"I have a video, a video she left you right before …"

"Before she died!" Amelia screamed.

"Before she ran away …" He whispered.

"Why would she run away?"

136

"Because she knew the truth about Cody and Elnora. She cracked." Rokas continued slowly.

"From now on you have to trust me, you got to calm down."

"Two minutes," Amelia instructed stiffly. "Two minutes then I'm gone." Rokas pushed himself up from the floor and resumed his seat. He then removed a small silvery camera-phone from under a cushion.

"Are you serious? A video? On that?" Amelia mocked. "I'm leaving." She snarled spitefully and walked towards the door. The sound of her name stopped her. She froze at the sound of her sister's voice. The voice was disturbed, clouded with static from a cheap mobile, but easy to identify.

"Amelia …" It chimed, marking itself in her mind forever.

§

Emma's Video Message.

"Amelia … if you are watching this now then you know. You know who we are. You know because you have been on a personal journey to uncover the truth." Tears trickled from Amelia's eyes, it sounded like Emma was in pain. "Because I went on that journey long before you, I always knew deep down they weren't our parents. I made contact with my father … our father, Rokas White, long ago. He told me everything. I told him how unhappy I was living with these people. I was in misery, always had been. I asked to him to fake my death. He organized it all, he was amazing. I had to put you through so much to get you here; I knew if I told you, you'd think I'd lost it. I needed to go into hiding, I'm in danger Amelia. I need to see you. I need to explain everything in great detail in person. I'm sorry for everything, but I know you will find it in your heart to forgive me. Rokas will bring you to me."

Emma stopped speaking and for the first time looked at the camera with forlorn eyes.

"I love you Amelia."

§

"You know what this means?" Amanda gulped, watching Rita Rose through the glass, nervously nibbling away at her already bitten nails.

"That Emma Gizzard is still alive?" Charles replied, his tone of voice shifting from relaxed to worried.

"Yes, Emma Gizzard is still alive."

"How did you know Rita was lying about the body being Emma's?"

"She confessed; came running in the other day in hysterics. Something's scared her."

"You don't think she did this as some sort of sick joke, you don't think Emma Gizzard is actually dead?"

"It's hard to say. Personally, if it's true, I'd say she was clearly forced to do it. I've never heard anything like it before. How could we be so stupid as to let something like that happen right under our noses? Do you realise what this will cause?" Charles shook his head in anger. "I think we should take Rita back to her cell, try again tomorrow."

"Good call, but for now I want everyone on the lookout for Emma and Amelia Gizzard."

"Amanda, Ron!"

A brunette haired woman suddenly came jogging up to them, her cheeks flushed.

"What is it, Mel?" Charles asked,

"It's June Gizzard." She cried, panting for breath. "What about her?" Amanda interjected.

"She's ... she's missing!"

§

Amelia began feeling nauseous. Before she knew it her stomach had wretched, warm bile spouting up her throat. She reached out for some stable support but fell to the floor.

"Amelia!" Rokas yelled, running to her aid.

"Get away from me!"

"Let me help you."

"All this time she was alive, and you let me suffer. My whole life is gone because of you!"

"Are you not happy she's alive?"

"Of course I'm happy!"

"Then what is it?"

Amelia's head dropped into her hands and she began crying.

"Don't cry."

"I ... I need to see her."

"Then I'll take you to her."

"Well, where is she?"

Rokas averted his eyes across the room for a few silent minutes. He swallowed before eventually turning to Amelia.

"She ... she's at Cody's house; she's been in his basement the whole time."

§

"The basement? But I was at Cody's a couple of months ago. The police would have been there searching; she would have been found?"

"No. She has an escape route if trouble is ever at the door," Rokas replied coolly.

"And what is it?"

"There's a small opening in the back wall she can just about fit through."

"A window?"

"Yes, a window."

"This can't be happening; I mean, it's not possible!"

"The world is full of surprises." Rokas whispered to himself.

"Tell me about it, look I can't waste any more time … I need to see her."

"I think you should rest first."

Amelia frowned. "I'll rest when I see Emma with my own eyes."

"Very well, but I need to know something?"

"What?" Amelia asked, all grouchy, her mind set on Emma.

"I need to know if you will … forgive me?"

Amelia sighed. "You will always be my Dad, I can't change that. Another thing I can't change is how I feel right now, how I've felt my whole life. I didn't do anything wrong, I just ended up in the wrong hands." She continued slowly. "I've wanted to kill you, but now we're here I don't think that's got to mean anything? This is my personal touchy stuff, stuff I'd never have dreamed of saying. But now I can, because once I see Emma, we're going to start a new life together. I don't care about June and I'm not going to cry over Elnora or Cody. This is my new chance, mine and Emma's new chance."

"So, what are you saying?"

"I … I can't forgive you Rokas, I could never forgive you for what you did to us and our mother. It's something you have to understand," she said kindly.

"I understand." He said blandly. "Come on, you've got a sister to see!"

§

"What are you having?" A cute waitress asked, her fingers clicking her pen every two to three seconds.

"I'll just have a coffee, and you?" Charles looked over at Amanda.

"I'll have the same."

"Why don't you have something to eat?" Charles suggested.

"No, I feel sick," she said bluntly.

"Just two coffees then?" The waitress asked Charles, trying to keep her eyes off a grumpy Amanda.

"Yes, thank you." He smiled politely.

The waitress strode off. After a couple of silent minutes, Ron transferred his focus to Amanda; her attention having switched to watching passing cars. He knew she was avoiding his attempt at caring.

"What's with you?" He suddenly blurted.

"Wh … what?"

"It's the case, isn't it?"

"I've failed her, I've failed Amelia."

"It's not your duty to look after her, you haven't even seen her in God knows how long."

"Oh, cut the shit will you? I told you she was innocent."

"How do we know that, she could have Emma right now?" Amanda tightened her fists in fury.

"Sod you!" She spat it out, angry.

"Why?"

"You irritate me and I don't know why. I feel like the world is against me. All because of you, you did this to me!" She cried.

"Keep your voice down!" Charles gestured with his hand, grateful the café was empty, not a soul in sight.

"Don't you dare tell me what to do; I wouldn't be here if I hadn't met you. Because of you I've been moved around the country more times than I can count. I don't have friends, my family don't speak to me … I don't know what to do." Amanda moaned, slumping back into her seat.

"I can tell you what to do," he said quickly.

"What?" They shared a slight pause before Charles leaned across and kissed her elegantly on the lips.

"Love me?" He begged. Her heart melted.

"Why should I?"

"Because I don't want you to feel like this any longer, I don't want to lose you again."

"Okay." She breathed, finally surrendering to the war that had been raging in her mind ever since she and Ron had lost touch.

"Really?"

"Yes." Her eyes glazed over. "I'll love you."

§

"Do you want me to come in with you?" Rokas asked.

"No, its better I see her alone."

"You're right." Rokas opened the car door. "Go on, go and see your sister."

Amelia slithered from the car; her breath misting up then quickly dissipating into the air. The door was ajar, as she'd expected. A layer of dust covered the walls inside. In the centre of the living room were a number of untouched dots of blood, fading. Cobwebs had taken ownership of every corner of every wall of every room, all adding to the 'abandoned' vibe of the house, despite it having been inhabited for several months by her sister; who, according to the rest of the world, was presumed dead.

Every time she'd visited the house she'd failed to discover that a basement even existed. Cody had never spoken of it. But this wasn't on her mind. Wasting no time she followed her orders. She had been briefed by

Rokas that pushing aside the washing machine in the wash room would uncover a gaping hole in the wall, which would lead her to a room with a single wooden door. She'd then enter that wooden door where she'd be welcomed by darkness, and a set of stairs. That set of stairs would take her to Emma.

Amelia crouched alongside the washing machine … her heart pumping. She thumped on her chest, coughing, clearing her lungs of dust and stale washing powder in the air. Using her shoulders she managed to move the heavy machine … success. Rokas hadn't misled her. Right where the machine had stood was a deep hole, evidently a passageway to a secret room. A room that had to be concealed would be a room of great importance. And so it proved. Crawling on hands and knees through dust and debris she feasted her eyes on the door she'd been so eager to pass through. Her key to freedom, the key she'd been waiting for. She turned the brass door handle; it opened slowly. A lone creak echoed in the darkness.
"Emma?" Amelia squeaked. A small whimpering noise bounced back to her from the top of the stairs. "Emma?" She repeated, this time more clearly. The whimpering noise gradually died down; then a shuffle and the sound of a light footstep.
"Am …Amelia?"

§

The light in the room flickered into life; the room much bigger than she'd assumed. Half the place had been taken over by rows of metal shelving filled with junk. The room was chilly; cold concrete walls and floors. Why had Cody hidden this room away?

Amelia was standing on the highest step; no support railings. Emma appeared from one of the shelves at the back of the room, wearing her shabby fabric cardigan with the odd tear or rip in places, her oily hair dangling down her back, her face coated in filth and grime. How had she survived in such conditions?

"Emma!" She gasped, flying down the stairs. Emma's eyes widened and she sprinted towards Amelia. Both shed tears as Emma dived into Amelia's outstretched arms.
"Am I dreaming?" Emma whispered.
"No, it's all okay now. I'm here." Amelia replied in between cheery sobs.
"Promise me you won't leave?"
"I promise, I'm here to stay!" Amelia felt warmth in her blood; nothing mattered anymore as long as she was with her sister.
"Come, we've got some talking to do." Amelia muttered softly after some minutes as she removed her sister's arms from around her neck.
"More time, I need more time."
"Okay." Amelia nodded, more tears.
"I need to tell you something." Emma said.
"What ..?"
Amelia was cut off; slowly she slid from her sister's arms and collapsed onto the concrete floor, gasping for breath. Realisation struck when she twisted her head to look up.
"Come on, look at me. I don't want you dead just yet." A voice hissed coldly. Emma loomed over her; in her right hand a thin carving knife, dripping Amelia's blood. On her face an evil crooked smile. Amelia sat upright struggling for leverage to stand. For her determined efforts she received a boot to the stomach, adding to the sharp pain already in her body.

"Yo … you stabbed me!" Amelia cried in disbelief.
"Yes, and there's plenty more to come."
"Why?" She asked in disbelief.
"Because it's what I've waited my whole life to do."
Emma stepped backwards, a menacing grin on her face.

§

"How could you do this, how could you stab me?"
Amelia exclaimed, coughing up blood. A minute ago
she'd been re-united with her sister. They'd shared a cry
and a hug … then her sister had brandished a thin
carving knife and driven it into her stomach.
"It was easy, really."
"Why, what did I ever do?"
"You know what you did!" Emma screamed, frantically
waving the knife in circles.
"You've lost it …"
"No, Amelia, I lost it years ago after what 'he' did to
me!"
"Who is 'he?"
"The bastard who raped me!" Amelia's jaw dropped,
her head pounding with guilt and misunderstanding.
"Who raped you?" She finally brought herself to ask.
"He didn't do it once, he did it every night."
It couldn't be …
"Oh, God, no!" Amelia heaved.
"Ryan Rain, also known as Cody Gizzard." Emma
shivered; tears of rage in her eyes. "You were always
asleep when he did it, all the times I cried, all the times I
said I hated him. You were too selfish to realise."
"So why me, why are you killing me?"
"Because you're the last on my list." Broken pieces of
her mind were gathering together, the picture becoming
clearer.

145

"You're the reason Cody and Elnora are dead, you're the reason June set me up." Amelia stated, barely able to believe she herself was accusing her sister of murder.
"Yes. It took some time to track Rokas down, but when I did, he confirmed he was my real father. I told him about the abuse and that I wanted Cody and Elnora dead, and as for June, she's the one who set you on the run, the one who made you think about your life. It was all organised."
"But, you didn't tell Rokas to kill me?"
"No, I wanted to kill you myself."
"Are you messing with my head?"
"No, this is all real."
"Oh, Emma …" Amelia sighed. "I'm sorry, I should have known."
"Yes, you should have, that's why you're here."
"You're wrong; I'm here to see my sister because I love her. Where is the sister I once knew? What have you become?"
"I was weak then, I'm strong now."
"No." Amelia laughed softly. "You're still weak."
"You forget, I can end your life in seconds." Emma said icily. "Anyway," she said loudly before Amelia could interrupt, "there's someone I want you to meet."

Across the room where the light had not reached, was a silhouette of June, arched over and looking very miserable. "Come here, June." Emma whispered, beckoning June with one hand. A nervous sweat broke out on her forehead; Amelia had discovered in the past that she certainly wasn't June's cup of tea.
"Here's the one." Emma spoke in a mothering voice, wrapping her arm around June's shoulders. "The one who made it all happen, my little soldier."
June nodded nervously.

"Your little soldier? Sorry, but it looks to me like she's almost … scared of you."

"You're not scared of me, are you baby?"

June shook her head emphatically, tears in her eyes. She still hadn't uttered a word.

"June, you don't have to be scared." Amelia said gently. "I understand now; how she made you do all that stuff, didn't she?"

June's eyes were bulging with panic.

"Look at her, your own daughter!"

"Be quiet!" Amelia jumped.

"I'll deal with you later." Emma whispered with an edge of threat to June "Did you bring it?"

"Y … yes."

"Well, come on then, we haven't got all day, where is it? Ah, yes, there we are." Emma grinned broadly as June slowly unwrapped a tacky dish cloth.

"You see Amelia." Emma diverted her focus from June. "I bet you can guess who June's father is?"

"C … Cody …" Amelia screamed in agony. If Emma didn't finish her off soon, her wound would.

"Where's the gun J ..?" Emma stopped at the touch of cold metal; a long object rested on the surface of her neck, digging into her skin.

"Y … you can't do it!" June said loudly in protest.

"Don't be an idiot June, lower the gun." Emma ordered through gritted teeth.

"You used me, you made me do things I didn't want to do! You sit there all day long criticizing Cody, Elnora and Amelia. You …you're as bad as them!"

"June, darling, it's okay … lower the gun." Emma whispered gently.

"Don't listen to her June!" Amelia cried.

"You be quiet, you piece of shit!" Emma retorted.

June's eyes swung back and forth between Emma and Amelia.

147

"You said yourself she's only using you June, don't let go of that gun or she'll kill us both!"

"I'm your Mum, June!" June shook her head in annoyance, then closed her eyes for thinking time.

"I'm sorry Mum," she finally said, "You need help, you're sick." With a groan of pain Amelia clambered upright, one hand clasping her wound. She hobbled over to Emma, keeping a safe distance.

"June, do you have your phone?" Amelia asked. "Yes, but it's in her pocket!"

"Why?"

"She told me to give it to her so she could ... record you dying." Amelia frowned in disgust.

"Give me the phone." She ordered Emma, standing still as a plank, a grimace on her face.

"Come and get it, I dare you." Emma growled.

"June I'm going to slowly reach into her pocket, if she makes one wrong move you shoot, okay?"

June nodded. Amelia wasn't convinced. She knew it wouldn't be much longer before Emma retaliated.

"Slowly ..."

Amelia crept forward, her eyes gazing nervously at June's gun. She could feel the denim as she reached into Emma's pocket, she was so close ...

§

SMACK.

Amelia tumbled backwards and chopped at the air with her arms in an attempt maintain stability. She staggered into one of the shelves which collapsed beneath her weight. Ancient papers and boxes scattered all over the room. Another crash bounced off the concrete walls as June came flying out of the dust and fell beside her.

"Where's the gun?" Emma screamed. Despite feeling close to death Amelia forced herself to concentrate; she wanted to stay alive rather longer. She peered over at

June who'd lost consciousness in the fall. A mist of dirt and dust had blanketed them, it was impossible to see where Emma was.

"June, come on. Wake up." Amelia hissed, shaking June with one hand. Emma's footsteps were becoming clearer as the seconds ticked by.

"Where's the gun?" Emma repeated. Amelia stopped shaking June's body. To her amazement, dangling elegantly from June's index finger was the gun. Shimmering silver. She could almost see her reflection. Cautiously Amelia wrapped her fingers firmly around the gun and struggled from the wreckage.

"Finally decided to show your face?" Emma said coolly as Amelia approached through the cloud of dust.

She has to die Amelia ...

"Where's June, dead I hope? Little traitor!"

Think of the sister you used to have, this one is only bringing pain to herself.

"I'm going to kill you Amelia." With tears blinding her eyes Amelia raised the gun.

"Wait, what are you doing?" Emma had suddenly lost the cool edge in her voice. An intense vibe filled the room, it was déjà vu. Except this time Emma was dying, and Amelia was pulling the trigger ...

"I'm sorry Emma, I'm sorry I couldn't protect you ..."

§

The sky was jewel blue, not a cloud. A fine summer's morning. The heavy sound of passing feet reminded her she'd be arriving any minute.

"I think that's her, at the end!" Amanda called out excitedly.

"I'm scared," Amelia whispered, heart thumping

"I understand. This must be so hard." Amanda stopped waving and turned, placing a hand tenderly on Amelia's shoulder.

"I knew it was Rokas, I knew all along." She looked over at the woman struggling through the crowds. "You say the word and I'll have him locked up." She said with reassurance.

"You know what this whole thing has taught me?"

"What?"

"That revenge … is not a good thing." Amelia laughed half-heartedly.

"You're right, Look I really should go." Amanda raised her arm to check her watch.

"What will you do now?"

Amanda frowned, almost as if the idea hadn't crossed her mind. "Well, I guess me and Charles will be settling down and carrying on from there."

"I'm glad you two are together, it feels right." Amelia smiled.

"Thank you for everything, Amanda."

"No, Amelia, thank you."

"For what?"

"For forgiving me. I should have found you sooner. Anyway," Amanda stared awkwardly at the floor, "Someone's here to see you." A thin woman finally appeared through the crowd; her long red hair streaked a pale grey, an unwelcome sign of ageing. Amanda said goodbye, and was gone. Amelia wondered if it was the last she'd ever see of Amanda McIsaac, she hoped not.

"Cecelia …"

"God, I haven't been called that in years, call me Deb."

"I've got something better, how about I call you Mum?" Amelia cried, flinging her arms around Deborah. As it turned out, her mother was none other than Deborah Fane. They'd met on the street, shared a conversation in the comfort of her living-room; she had spoken to her mother without realising.

"I'm sorry, for everything." Her mother said gently once they'd found their emotional grip. They stood at the door of St. Pauls Cathedral.

"You don't need to be sorry, it was him!" Amelia protested. "The one thing I don't understand is, why? Why did he take us?"

"Greed, anger, spite. Fate has a funny way of working." Deborah sighed. "Amanda told me you've been talking to a psychiatrist?

"Yes, but I'll be leaving him soon."

"Why?"

"Because …" Amelia took a steady breath. "I'm moving."

"Where?"

"New York."

"That's great!" Deborah exclaimed.

"No, it's not."

"How so?"

"Because it means I'll be leaving. I've only just found you."

"No!" Deborah cried, shaking her head. "Don't worry about me."

"I can't leave you …"

"Yes, you can." She assured Amelia, softly, cupping her cheeks in warm hands.

§

When Amelia had squeezed the trigger she'd opened the door to a meaningful life. The police had burst in at the scene of Emma's corpse and June's unconscious body. In Amelia's eyes it had come across as 'finishing them off'. But once June had opened her mouth the truth had come out. The world had no sooner learnt Amelia had been framed and nearly killed in her battle for freedom, than she was crowned a hero by both those who knew her well and those who didn't. Occasionally she'd hear 'I think it's a lie, I think she killed them all.' But her worries had slipped away the moment she'd walked free from the courts.

Sadly, after these tragic events life held little happiness for Amelia, at first bedridden by internal conflict, guilt and anger. Her sister had been abused sexually throughout her childhood; June's father was Cody ... the man who'd taken Amelia and Emma and named them as his 'own.' But now a bright light shone for her, a glimmering future which she would take by the hands. Life wasn't so bad anymore when Amelia thought about it. She now had hope and a real mother, even if they were continents apart. June. on the other hand was finding life a constant obstacle, but no matter what anyone thought, Amelia knew that deep down the girl had a strong soul, one day she'd find that bright light.

Amelia took the letter Elnora had given her before passing away; she'd promised herself that once she was free she'd open it. But now that she was free the letter held no interest, she didn't want more from the past. She calmly shredded it into tiny pieces.
"Goodbye, Elnora." The pieces spread across the pavement like confetti. Amelia gazed at them for a few seconds then wiped her face on her sleeves, before turning to her mother. "What now?"
"When do you leave for New
York?"
"Tomorrow, why?"
"Well, then you have time for a quick drink, don't you?" Deborah chuckled, linking arms with Amelia.
"Yes." Amelia beamed happily. "I do."

www.ingramcontent.com/pod-product-compliance
Lightning Source LLC
Chambersburg PA
CBHW070933130626
46555CB00001B/412